TRAFFICKED SERIES

By: Taylor Ann Stone

Table of content

Part 1 1

CHAPTER 1 2
CHAPTER 2 14
CHAPTER 3 25
CHAPTER 4 31
CHAPTER 5 35
CHAPTER 6 42
CHAPTER 7 54
CHAPTER 8 60
CHAPTER 9 66
CHAPTER 10 74
CHAPTER 11 79
CHAPTER 12 85
CHAPTER 13 88
CHAPTER 14 95
CHAPTER 15 103

Part II 108

CHAPTER 16 109
CHAPTER 17 117
CHAPTER 18 122
CHAPTER 19 128
CHAPTER 20 141
CHAPTER 21 157

CHAPTER 22 164
CHAPTER 23 169
CHAPTER 24 171
CHAPTER 25 177
CHAPTER 26 183
CHAPTER 27 186
CHAPTER 28 191
CHAPTER 29 198
CHAPTER 30 203
CHAPTER 31 208
CHAPTER 32 216
CHAPTER 33 222
CHAPTER 34 227
CHAPTER 35 231
CHAPTER 36 236
CHAPTER 37 240
CHAPTER 38 244
CHAPTER 39 254

Part 1

CHAPTER 1

Adeline knelt on the slick hallway floors picking up her science textbook that laid in a pile of her other books and loose papers splayed all around her. A long, brown tendril of hair covered the sadness in her eyes as the humiliation burned into her cheeks. Students changing classes walked around her, kicking her papers as they passed by. She scrambled to retrieve them and remove the dirty black shoe prints.

Monica, Lucy, and I rounded the corner heading to the cafeteria, and witnessed the event as it ended. I was embarrassed for Adeline and then angry. Janis Stapleton, Katie Becker, and Trishelle Ronan kept walking, snickering and laughing at the poor girl's misfortune. High school humiliation could be brutal, especially as the victim of bullying. It had been a long time since I was bullied myself, but I never forgot the trauma.

The incident replayed itself in my head and I saw Janis push Adeline out of her way knocking her backpack off her shoulder and dumping its contents on the ground. The trigger inside me that sensed injustice went off. What was happening to Adeline wasn't fair. I remembered so clearly when I was her, standing there while other kids laughed and pointed. My empathy for Adeline grew almost as much as my rage for Janis. Adeline was a beautiful soul from what I knew about her. She was a quiet girl with long, red hair and freckles sprinkling the bridge of her nose. I never really saw her interact with many people and didn't notice whether or not she had friends, but I knew she was smart. I got paired up with her once in biology and she helped me ace our midterm exam.

I sped up until I reached Adeline, knelt down, and began

picking up her books. "Here, let me help you."

She said nothing. I tried to make eye contact, but she kept her gaze lowered to the floor. A tear fell down her cheek as she nodded in silent appreciation, slowly gathering the rest of her papers. Her shoulders were slumped and defeated and the wrinkles in her scrunched brow indicated the emotional pain she was enduring was intense. All I could think about was Adeline going home today and having to tell her mom what happened to her again.

Janis and her cronies were smirking and laughing as they walked off. Anger surged through my veins, pumping renewed hatred for her. The audacity of Janis to think she could push others around and get away with it just because she was considered the most popular girl in school. As last year's homecoming queen and likely this year's prom queen, she had an entitled attitude unparalleled in the history of stuck up, rich, popular cheerleaders.

I looked up and glared at her as she walked down the hall

away from me.

"Don't let her get you you, Adeline. She's a miserable witch. I'm surprised she doesn't park her broom in the senior parking lot."

She didn't respond, instead, SHE picked up the last of her books, crammed them into her backpack, and wiped her face.

Adeline was far too submissive to do anything about this. One look at her body language and it was obvious. She was resigned to believe that this was her lot in life, something she'd have to accept. It was sad to watch her so defeated. It looked like I was the one who's going to have to stand up to Janis. She'd ramped up her bullying lately and it had gotten out of hand. Somebody had to put a stop to it.

I stood up, turned around to see her as she and her friends walked down the hall. "Hey Janis!"

She stopped, turned around, and looked at me with a quizzical brow.

Adeline grabbed my hand. "No, please. You'll just make it worse."

Janis saw me and narrowed her eyes. She looked to her friends on the left and right of her then started walking toward me. Her posture and body language were confrontational. As far as any bystander could tell, I was stoic, my chin held high in defiance. She wasn't going to get away with this. I waited for her to get within range of hearing me without having to shout at her. "I think you owe Adeline an apology."

Janis looked at her friends and then gave me a look that was curious to know if I was serious. I matched her look with one of my own that told her I was. Adeline stood there, her eyes bulging in terror.

Janis and I had a long history that started in third grade when we were best friends. I was there for her when her parents divorced. Her father decided that holidays were better spent with his mistress and trips to Aspen while her mother got more plastic surgery and drowned her depression in Jack Daniels.

Evan Keller was the only boy that Janis lived and died for in the seventh grade. She followed him around for weeks, hiding any time he would look in her direction. So she was heartbroken when Evan asked me to the Halloween dance instead of her. I turned him down but she didn't believe me when I told her I had no interest in him. Then challenged me to a fight on the football field after school. The whole school showed up. I met her out there to try and talk her out of it, but when she tried to throw a punch, I used the combat techniques my father taught me to block it sending her face first on the cold concrete scabbing her elbows and knees. Since that day, we haven't spoken, adopting a "live and let live" philosophy.

Janis was never alone, in fact, she always had Katie and Trishelle by her side, egging her on and applauding her behavior. Today was no different. I looked each of them in the eyes, "do you want some of what some of what she's

7

got coming?" I pointed to Janis, my intention was to put them both on the defensive and get them to back off so that I could square off with Janis alone. It worked. They saw how serious I was and shifted their gazes to the floor before retreating and walking down the hallway.

Unfortunately, there are rich kids like Janis at this private school who prey on others for sport. They were cowards though, and I have no problem telling them exactly where they can go. They don't intimidate me. I am well liked for my ability to like just about anyone I come into contact with, mostly because I stand up for others who can't stand up for themselves. Janis and her mean girls make life miserable for everybody.

Adeline had been Janis' favorite victim from what I had witnessed. Mostly because she was quiet and didn't fight back. But bullies like Janis didn't learn by their victims backing down from her.

"What business is it of yours?" She sneered.

An audience was growing and reminded me of junior high all over again. I didn't particularly want an audience but it was too late now.

"It's everybody's business, Janis. Kids are tired of your bullying." I replied.

She moved closer, entering into my personal space. "I don't know what you're talking about. I don't bully anyone. I simply bumped into her by accident." The corner of her mouth upturned in a feigned smile.

In recent years, the term "bully" has been considered very taboo and anyone labeled a bully considered a horrible person. It was obvious Janis didn't want to be labeled a bully, but she sure was behaving like one. I took a step toward her, closing the distance between us to show her I wasn't afraid of her. "Maybe you should watch where you're going from now on. Otherwise, it may not be too long before someone bumps into you."

I waited for her response. But instead of hitting or

screaming at me, she backed down. It wasn't the reaction I was expecting. She probably noticed that the crowd was growing and reminded her that history could very well repeat itself if she wasn't careful. Janis turned around and headed down the hallway catching up to Katie and Trishelle. They turned the corner and were out of sight.

The crowd gave a few laughs and dispersed. I took a deep breath and turned around and looked at Adeline. Her facial expression was stuck in a state of shock as her red hair draped over her left eye. "H-how did you do that?" She asked.

"You should try it sometime. You might like it." I winked and smiled. My first inclination was to give her advice about how to handle Janis or any other bully in the future, but I didn't. She was so timid and mild mannered that I wasn't sure that my advice would just go straight through her ears and out the other side.

"I couldn't." Adeline protested.

"Listen, they prey on your fear. If you give into them then they take it as weakness." I argued.

Adeline shrugged her shoulders, nodding her head in understanding.

I sighed knowing nothing would change. There was nothing I could do if she wouldn't stand up for herself. Still, was it worth the effort and frustration to try and convince her or just let her walk away?

I decided that it was best to let her make her own decisions. Perhaps I'd invite her over to my house later in the week. Maybe by befriending her, it would pump up her confidence eventually.

"Thank you, Marnie." Adeline smiled.

"Anytime." I replied.

She walked away. I watched her disappointed with her lack of conviction but determined to keep my optimism about the situation.

"Hey girlie. You know you're a badass, right?" Monica Brewster peeked her head around the corner.

"Yeah, Janis had better watch her back. Did you see how fast she backed down from you?" Julie Plier stood next to Monica.

"Thanks guys." I smiled.

"You know you're the coolest person around these parts, right?" Monica smiled.

"I know I have the coolest friends at least." I said.

It was nice of them to say, but I think if I were really that cool of a person then I would have found a way to get Adaline to stand up for herself. Sadly, it's unlikely anything will change with Adeline. Logically, I know I can't accept responsibility for Adeline on myself, but it was hard not to feel responsible for the innocent girl.

"You've got to know that Adeline appreciated what you did for her, right?" Lucy asked me.

"Yeah, I just wish she would have done it for herself," I replied.

Lucy interrupted. "There's nothing any of us can do if she won't stand up for herself."

"I guess." My face conveyed my disappointment. It was still worth the effort and frustration to stand up against Janis because I know that she's been taunting other kids around the school. It was time to give her a warning shot across the bow anyhow and let her know that her behavior was going to be tolerated much longer.

"I'm starving," Monica said. "Let's head to lunch, okay?"

I nodded my head and let Lucy and Monica lead the way. I figured I could use something to eat before math class.

We passed by Janis again. This time she was in her little girl squad group giving us the side eye as we passed. I didn't say anything to her but I gave her a look that let her know that today was not the day to push me.

We made our way to the cafeteria, found our usual table,

and sat down around it.

I expected that Janis was going to try to get some sort of retaliation later in some underhanded way, but for right now I was just going to focus on my meatloaf.

CHAPTER 2

All the drama with Janice made me almost forget that I love coming to sixth period Math. Not because I enjoyed the subject matter. In fact, it was really boring and Mister Roberts was about the worst teacher. He had a low monotone voice that rarely rose above a quiet whisper making it nearly impossible not to fall asleep in his class. I often wondered if they sent these Math teachers to some conference and taught them how to be intentionally boring. Maybe there was a huge conspiracy with China to fail American students so we'd have no choice but to admit that China was far superior in arithmetic.

Putting that aside, sixth period Math was when I got to see Dmitri Holin. Hands down the hottest guy at our school and a recent transfer student from Russia. His thick strong accent still echoed in my head from the first time he said hello. It's the kind of accent that instantly has you in the middle of a spy movie starring as the sexy vixen in your own mind. Every morning I'd notice that his parents dropped him off at the front of the school. He'd step out of their Mercedes Benz in a black wool trench coat, slicked coal black hair and emerald green eyes burning into the soul of every girl who was within a five meter radius of his presence. I wasn't immune to his great looks or mysterious attraction. I absolutely wanted him to notice me.

He'd joined the swim team and I'd heard that he was really

good. Kids were already talking about him. Without a doubt, Dmitri was the most eligible bachelor in our school.

"Hey Marnie." A voice from behind me radiated a little too much enthusiasm. When I turned around I noticed a familiar face. It was Alex Barnett. Captain of the football team, baseball team, and pretty much an all around jerk. He'd been trying to sleep with me since freshman year when he heard I was one of the last living virgins apparently.

"What's up, Alex." I didn't wait for his response. I walked into the classroom fixing my eyes on Dmitri already sitting in his seat.

I don't know who in the heavens above put in a good word for me, but the fates had arranged for Dmitri's assigned seat to be directly behind mine.

"Uh, wait. You got a minute?" Alex followed behind me. Unfortunately, he was also in my math class and spent most of his time trying to get my attention.

16

"Not really, Alex. Mr. Roberts doesn't like us to be tardy." Alex was about to say something else but thought better of it and instead found his seat.

I walked toward Dmitri in my most sultry walk I could expect from my gangly legs and when I was at my seat, I gave a subtle hair flip and turned around, bending over just enough that my mini skirt hiked itself up to my mid hamstring right before sitting down.

"My mom won't be home for hours today. What do ya'll say we take her credit card and go shopping?" Monica had a serious shopping addiction. It was all Lucy and I could do not to look at each other because we knew where this could go if we enabled her behavior.

"Last time we went shopping, we ended up having to get after school jobs to pay back all the money you charged up." Lucy accused. I just laughed.

I tried to subtly turn my head around to see if Dmitri was looking at me and when I did I caught his piercing gaze.

His eyes bore into mine and I suddenly felt very aware of how close in proximity we were to each other.

Very few people knew much about him. I know because I asked almost everyone in the school. The only thing anyone knew was that he moved here from Russia because both of his parents worked at the embassy.

I turned my attention back to the front of the class. Mr. Roberts had started talking and the room grew silent. I could feel the heat of his body blazing against my back and the sensation sent tingles throughout my entire body. Looking at him was almost pleasurably painful. It hurt so good. I'd never seen another guy in my life with black hair and green eyes. He was cool and aloof at the same time which only served to antagonize his mystery factor. Every girl in our school wanted him and I was no exception. However, I wasn't about to throw myself at him. I had self-respect and standards. I knew that a guy like Dmitri wouldn't waste his time on a girl who was easy to get. Why would he when he had any girl around to choose from the crowd?

I played like I wasn't interested even though deep down I got chills every time I heard his voice. When Mr. Roberts called his name, panic in my body sent waves of fire lapping at the deepest, darkest primal parts of me. He didn't seem like he even belonged in high school. He acted so much older. When he was around I'd try to dance a balance of making eye contact with him without it seeming obvious or too forward. It didn't seem to matter how cool I acted. I had a feeling he could see straight into my soul and knew that I wanted him.

He had a slender muscular build that made it very easy for a girl like me to imagine what it would be like to get tangled in those arms. His chiseled facial features and slight stubble made me imagine what it would be like to rub my cheek against his chin in the throes of passion.

Three months had gone by since school started and Dmitri had arrived. That was three months of playing coy and trying not to have him notice that I was noticing him. I was done hiding and playing. Every time we'd managed to say a few words to each other it was mostly about asking me a question about math. Quite frankly, I couldn't care less about any equations except for me plus him equaling eternal bliss.

Mr. Roberts turned the lights off and turned on his projector. He was about to demonstrate another formula for us.

I felt my blonde hair being pushed to the side and then a thick Russian accent whispered in my ear. The air of his breath tickled my lobe. "Any plans today after school?"

My breath caught in my throat. I thought it was a very forward question since I had barely spoken more than ten words to him in the whole time that he'd been at the school. But I didn't care. He knew what he was doing. He knew that approaching me that way would turn me on, and knowing that he knew how to turn me on made me even more turned on.

The sexual tension was palpable and for a second I was worried that everyone else in the class could sense it, but they seemed not to notice. Then it felt like a secret between him and I. Something we shared and kept within ourselves. I'd just talked with Monica and Lucy about doing something with them today, but if Dmitri wanted to do something I was a solid yes. I knew my girls would understand in a heartbeat.

I didn't answer him right away, still trying to play my hand cool and calm. I didn't want him to know I was eager to jump his bones. Instead, I waited a beat or two before whispering, "maybe."

"Wanna come over to my place and hang out?" This time the top of his head nuzzled the back of mine, the dark classroom hiding our intimate exchange.

There it was. The invitation that any girl would die to get- - laid out on a platter for me to accept. I didn't want to show my enthusiasm. Let's face it. The guy was gorgeous and he knew it. He also knew that he could have handed that invitation to any girl in this classroom and they would have fought each other like animals to be the last one standing and the object of his affection.

"Perhaps. I'll let you know after seventh period."

"Don't keep me waiting too long, Marnie." I heard him lean back in his chair.

Did this just happen? I couldn't wait to get out of class. Monica and Lucy were going to die! I wanted to scream as loud as I could like a five year old girl. So when the bell finally rang, I got out of there fast and waited for them to meet me in the hall.

"What's the hurry?" Lucy said.

I grabbed both of them by the arm and pulled them into the lady's bathroom. I checked to make sure no one else was in the stall. "You're *never* going to believe this!" I screamed.

"What's going on?" Monica put her hand on my shoulder.

"Dmitri just asked me over to his house today." My eyes bulged out of my head and my mouth dropped open as I awaited their response.

"Shut right up!" Lucy looked like she'd been hit by a truck. She was one of the girls in school that was in love with him. However, I knew that she would be happy for me. He was fair game and any one of us would have been happy for the other if he'd picked her.

"Are you kidding me?" Monica followed on Lucy's shock. "When? When did he ask you?"

"Last period." I had to admit it felt good to be the center of envy for once. "We're going to have to postpone our plans, is that okay?" I asked.

Both Monica and Lucy gave me a condescending look and then Monica answered for both of them. "Uh, yeah. I'd kick your butt if you didn't!"

"You've got to do it," Lucy said. "You would be doing this

for every girl at Emory Academy."

"Let's not be so dramatic," I laughed.

"It's a no-brainer. You have to tell us every single detail and not leave anything out. Do you understand?" Lucy grilled.

"A nice girl doesn't kiss and tell." I teased.

"Good thing you're not a nice girl." Monica snickered.

"Okay, well I'll catch up with you later." I walked to my next class in a complete daze and completely unable to think about anything but that tall, dark Russian who I would be making out with in less than two hours. Definitely an experience I'll never forget.

CHAPTER 3

"Mom, I'm going to have dinner at Monica's tonight and then we're going to catch a movie." I wait for her voice on the other end of the line to tell me it's okay.

"Sure sweetheart. Don't be home too late. Your father and I have to work late tonight anyway."

Monica's parents are always inviting me over so it isn't out of the ordinary. I wish I could say that I felt guilty about lying to her, but I didn't. My parents have always been strict with me and if I had told her the truth she never would have let me go over to a boy's house even if his parents were home. They were both extremely old-fashioned and it was like breaking into a bank just to get a few freedoms. I figured what they didn't know wouldn't hurt them and I wasn't going to stay out late. Besides, if I missed this chance, I knew there were a line of girls waiting to have a chance with him.

I hung up the phone and excitedly ran over to my mirror, dancing and jumping up and down to the latest hit on the radio. I had to wear my hair down and find something in my closet that didn't make me look like a child. As I yanked each hanger in my closet from left to right looking for the perfect outfit, I kept thinking about his exotic accent. My knees threatened to buckle just thinking about him.

I pushed my breasts up in a pink v-neck sweater and added blush to my cheeks and lipstick on my mouth. I gave my hair a final look before heading out the door. On the way out Chester keeps barking. "What's the matter, boy? You miss me today?" Chester was approaching 14 years old. He was useless as a security guard but he was a great friend otherwise.

I gave him a treat, scratched behind his ears before grabbing my keys and walking out the door. I pushed the button on my keychain and unlocked my white Mercedes before grabbing the handle and getting in. My parents got me this car for my 17th birthday. It was an unexpected gift and I was grateful for it. A thought entered my brain-- I wonder if I could start giving Adeline a ride to school from now on? Maybe I could build a rapport with her and she might start standing up for herself.

I'd have to think about that later. Right now, I was too excited about my date with Dmitri. I backed out of the driveway and stopped briefly to put his address in my phone. Funny enough, he only lived a couple of streets away. It wasn't really a coincidence. Government employees who worked with the embassy usually lived in adjacent neighborhoods.

I turned the radio up feeling my look and the excitement of what was about to happen. Soon I was at his house and pulled into his driveway. I walked up to the door and rang the bell.

Dmitri answered the door wearing a black button down shirt and a pair of blue jeans. He must have changed since seeing him at school and he smelled of fresh cologne. "Welcome, beautiful. Please come in."

I walked into a beautiful and enormous house. White modern furniture lined the walls and complemented the large, white tiles that covered the foyer. "You have a beautiful home." My voice wavered, betraying my nervousness.

Dmitri grabbed my hand and led me up the staircase. "Follow me."

I hesitated, suddenly unsure of myself. He must have sensed it because he stopped, turned around to face me, and kissed me gently. It felt good to have the heat of his breath against my lips. "Where are your parents?" I asked.

"They're still at work. Don't worry. We have plenty of time." His confidence helped support mine and I followed him up the stairs and into his room.

He stopped when he got to the door and waited for me. "Are you nervous?"

I looked him square in the eyes, "should I be?"

"No. Not with me." He opened the door to his room and it was massive. He had his own private bathroom that looked like the size of my kitchen.

"Wow this is amaz-" he covered my mouth with his own.

This was the moment I'd been excited about. I couldn't wait to tell Monica and Julie. His lips felt warm and inviting and I allowed myself to relax into the experience. The way he flicked and moved his tongue around my mouth was intoxicating.

My thighs set fire and my belly tingled. I craved to be closer to him.

He led me to the bed where we continued kissing. He stopped for a second, held my face in his hands. "Marnie, what happens here stays here. No one at school will know. This is just for us two." He reached for the strings on my shirt and untied them, releasing the fabric. He unbuttoned the front of my blouse and exposed my bare breasts. His mouth then traveled to my neck where he placed a series of small kisses before making his way to the outline of my chin.

I met his mouth with mine and our kisses became hotter and more passionate. I wrapped my arms around his neck and pulled him closer to me. He stood up and took his shirt off. I reached for the button of his pants and started to unzip them when we heard the doorknob turn and two voices talking. A man and a woman walked in.

I froze, humiliation burning in my cheeks.

They casually spoke to him in Russian before they realized what was happening. When the woman turned and saw us there, she said something to her husband which led them both to back out of the room. She said something to Dmitri that I couldn't make out and then gave me a half smile before closing the door behind them both.

"Your parents, I presume?" I tried not to sound as caught off guard and humiliated as I was but I failed. The situation was awkward and I had no idea how I would face his parents after this.

He kissed my hand and said something in Russian to me, which despite my embarrassment, reignited my desire for him.

"Get dressed," he said. "Let's get something to eat."

CHAPTER 4

His parents' awkward smile made me uncomfortable. I felt like they should have been more upset than they were. And Dmitri, too. He handled it calmly. Too calmly. There was no embarrassment from his end either. They were all handling the situation with extreme maturity. It was confusing. I expected his mother to scream bloody murder and call me a trollop before shoving me out the front door with only my humiliation to comfort me. Maybe it was a cultural thing? Perhaps where they come from sex isn't as big a taboo as we Americans treat it.

And what was with them being home? I thought they were still at work. I wasn't exactly going to win the award for most wholesome girlfriend in the world.

"I'll give you a minute. When you're ready, join me downstairs." He walked out of the door.

I buttoned my blouse and tied the strings. I'd rather have Janis smash my face into the cafeteria trash can than walk

32

past his parents right now. Unfortunately, I couldn't hide up here in Dmitri's room all night either. I inhaled a couple of deep breaths before exhaling forcefully. I stood up and walked out of the room, down the stairs and into what appeared to be the dining room where Dmitri and his parents sat. "I-I'm really sorry about earlier," I stammered.

"Would you like to join us for dinner?" His mother asked.

That caught me off-guard. "I'd be delighted, thank you." That took some relief off of me and for a moment I felt like everything would be alright.

Dmitri was to my right and he gave me a sweet smile. I pictured what my life would be like as Dmitri's girlfriend. Accepted into his family and on his arm for the whole school to envy. As I was a full tilt in my daydream, their help brought out the food. "This looks delicious, Mrs. Holin."

"Please, call me Patricia." Her accent was almost as thick as Dmitri's. "We have plenty so let's eat up!"

I was served a big plate of pasta with alfredo sauce. I picked up the fork next to me and dug into the pile of noodles, twisting it around and then inserting it into my mouth. There was something especially delicious about this dish. I couldn't quite place the ingredient that was a combination of tangy and sweet. It was amazing and I'd never had alfredo pasta this good. Before I'd realized it, I'd finished my plate.

"Would you like more, dear?" Patricia's question was innocent enough but her facial expression hinted to something darker.

"I'm full, thank you. It was delicious."

"Thank you. Mr. Holin brought the recipe back from Russia on his last trip."

"So what did you kids have planned for this evening?" Mr. Holin asked.

I looked to Dmitri for an answer to his father's question when he began looking at me strangely. "Are you feeling alright?"

At first, I didn't realize what he was referring to, but then I noticed that my eyelids were dragging. I tried to answer him but my speech slurred as I spoke. "Where's the bath-bathroom?"

"Around the corner," Patricia pointed.

I stumbled away from the table and around the corner heading toward the bathroom when my vision blurred blocking my ability to see. I fell to the floor and the last thing I remember was falling to the ground. Everything went black.

CHAPTER 5

Something in the faint distance nudged my conscience awake. I tried to open my eyes but was distracted by the relentless pain jackhammering its way across my frontal lobe.I pressed my hand to my head to find that my hair was damp and stringy. I couldn't remember anything. A noise coordinated with the movement of my hand and I realized something was around my wrists. Squeezing my eyes shut in an effort to get my eyes to focus, I opened them again to see the same dark room. I adjusted my legs as I sat up and realized I had shackles around my wrists and ankles. The cold concrete floor laid against the back of my thighs and I noticed I wasn't wearing any pants. Looking down I noticed I wasn't wearing anything but my bra and underwear. Panic gripped me. How did I get here? Who put me here? Tears flooded down my cheeks. "Help! Help! Somebody, please help me!"

"Shut up! You'll get us all in trouble." A feminine whisper echoed in the dark room. Her voice was shaky and low. As my eyes focused, I could see a slight outline of a figure sitting against the wall with a small, rectangular window overhead. I couldn't see out but I could tell it was night outside.

From the mildew smell, the closest I could guess was that we were in a basement. It would explain the cold, wet feeling. I continued to try to make out what the rest of the room looked like when I heard several other voices, coughing or crying all in various levels of sound but all with a touch of fear in their voices. I turned my head back to the voice that spoke out to me earlier. "Where are we?"

"Shhhh!" She snapped at me.

A series of footsteps above our heads shifted. The blood in my veins grew cold as I heard them get closer to our location. Then a light turned on and I gasped. There were at least 20 women tied to the wall in the same shackles I was wearing. They all tried to shield their eyes from the fluorescent light of the basement. The women appeared to know what the sound meant because they all got very quiet. There was the sound of a door creaking open and then silence for what seemed like forever before the door shut again and the light followed.

It was terrifying. The women seemed to collectively gasp in relief. "What's going on? How long have I been here?" I whispered. Where was Dmitri? Where were his parents? And how did I get here?

The girl who spoke to me before tried to keep her voice low. "A couple of days ago they brought you in here with us."

"Who? Who brought me here?" I asked.

"The family upstairs." Her voice was a little stronger this time through the dark. "The husband and wife and son."

I took a second to let her words sink into my brain. Dmitri's family? Could this be possible? My mind races trying to recall any warning signs that I should have seen. The last thing I remember was sitting at their dining table eating before I felt nauseous. Could they have poisoned me? This felt like something straight out of a horror movie. How could this happen?

"Is there any way out of here?" I asked.

"If there were, do you think we'd all still be here?" Her Brooklyn accent was more present in her speech this time.

"What are we going to do?" I cried.

"The only thing we can do- survive." I could see the outline of her lean toward me. "Just stay quiet and do what they say."

"How long have you been here?" I stifled my sobs trying to act braver than I felt.

"I'm not sure; a few weeks I think." She answered. "That's my best guess."

"Have you tried to escape?" I wondered what these girls had already tried.

"Of course we've tried. But the basement window has bars in front of it and the walls are reinforced with soundproof foam. There's no way out and no one to hear us."

I let her last words linger in my ears. No way out? What does that mean? What would Dmitri's family mean to do with so many of us? "Has anyone ever left?"

"Yeah, all the time actually. They come down and blindfold a handful of girls, take them out of here and we never see them again." The girl scooches down onto the floor in the prone position.

"What does that mean?" Panic re-emerged in my body.

"The best we can figure it, they're trafficking us." She said this so matter-of-factly that I didn't grasp the weight of her words at first.

"Trafficking? What do you mean?" I asked.

"How old are you, girl?" Her tone turned condescending.

"Seventeen," I answered.

"Oh, another young one. Damn." There was a faint hint of pity in her words. "Look, I don't know how to tell you this, but you're going to be sold soon."

"Sold?" Her words shocked me. "As in like a slave?"

"Yeah," she adjusted her body to a better sleeping position. "All you can do is obey what they tell you to do and wait. At least you'll get out of here at some point." She turned her back to me and didn't say another word.

Why did she appear so calm? Had she been down here long enough to accept her fate? My mind ran the previous list of events that had occurred. Seeing Dmitri at school, flirting with him and lying to my parents about meeting him. Oh no. My parents. They don't know where I am. They must be so worried by now. A surge of guilt overtook me and I buried my face in my hands. The cold metal of the shackles bruised my wrists. I lied to my parents and now they have no clue where I am.

Who were Dmitri and his parents? Did they really work at the embassy? And how was I going to find my way out of this situation? I laid on the cold floor, tucking my knees

41

into my chest and crying silently as I heard faint sounds of heartbreak that matched my own.

CHAPTER 6

A single stream of light infiltrated the basement window and pierced my eyelid. I squinted and moved my head which woke me up just as the door at the top of the stairs creaked open and a man's voice yelled down to us speaking Russian. Based on the tone of his voice, it seemed he wanted us to wake up and move quickly. I wasn't inclined to comply but I was also still terrified. I didn't know who this guy was or what he was capable of doing to me. The daylight illuminated the basement and I was shocked to see so many girls down here. Last night, I couldn't see them even though I heard several of them wailing and talking to each other. You couldn't see your hand in front of your face when the lights were out.

I sat up and watched as the other girls got up and looked at him. He pointed to me and four other girls and motioned for us to follow him upstairs. "What's going on? Why did he point at me?" Panic ripped through my veins.

"It's time for bathroom breaks and breakfast." The girl from last night ran her fingers through her dark wavy hair in an attempt to brush out any minor tangles. "We're going first."

It was a bit remarkable how nonchalant most of these girls were acting about the situation. They were covered in dirt and grime, sleeping on the cold concrete and most of them looked like this was a normal morning for them.

One girl, in particular, looked no older than fifteen years old. Her small frame shook from the morning chill in the air. She wore jean shorts and a white tank top that looked like it hadn't been washed in a month. Her long caramel hair was tangled and stuck to the back of her head. She broke my heart.

A desperate thought plowed through my brain. Had they been down here that long that they'd come to accept their fate? And would I do the same? I prayed a silent prayer for God to help me out of this situation, promising never to go anywhere without a chaperone again.

"What's waiting for us at the top of the stairs?" I asked her.

"It's fine. Just follow me and you'll be okay."

"How long have you been-" the tubby, balding Russian interrupted me. He yelled what could only be described as a stream of Russian curse words while pointing a finger in my face. I assumed it meant that I should stop talking. We made eye contact and the seriousness in his facial expressions told me that I'd better comply.

The girl I was talking to nodded her head to the man in agreement. She placed her hand on the middle of my back and gently pushed me up the stairs. My bare feet jerked at the wood step underneath and the hint of a small splinter that almost impaled my big toe. I adjusted my foot and stepped up. The wood underneath my foot threatened to break, but I ignored it and walked up each step with intention and speed. I made my way up the stairs until I was through the door and into what looked to be the kitchen. My eyes burned and I squinted to deny some of the bright lights to enter into them. My hand protected my face while I waited a few seconds for them to adjust.

The other three girls that were chosen with us fell into step behind this girl and myself. Together we all made it to the central part of the house. I could see Dimitri's parents intensely staring at a huge computer monitor. There were several black monitors circling the big central one on a large desk. They were speaking to each other in Russian and pointing to what looked to be photographs on the screens.

The bald tubby man pointed to my new friend, spoke something in Russian and motioned to her, and then pointed to the rest of us. I assumed it meant that he wanted her to manage the bathroom breaks for the rest of us. She nodded. "Okay, we have to hurry up." She said.

"How do you know what he's saying?" I asked.

"I've done this routine long enough. He puts me in charge so he can go into the kitchen and stuff his face with danish pastries."

She didn't seem particularly bothered by the situation. My attention turned back to a few seconds ago and the way they were looking at the computer screens. I wondered what they were looking at. I only got a glimpse of black and white pictures on the screen. One side of the screens seemed to show surveillance footage from multiple angles. Were they surveilling the outside of the house? It would make sense. If they were trying to keep this many girls captive, they'd probably take that kind of precaution to keep anyone who might come to the door out.

 The girl moved us across from the kitchen and into a giant guest bathroom that was bigger than my bedroom. A crystal chandelier hung from the highest point of the ceiling in the middle of the room. There was a double vanity with fuschia vinyl high back chairs pushed neatly under them and mirrors that stretched from the vanity to the top of the ceiling. The entire house mimicked this type of luxury. It made sense to me that they would be able to keep a lot of women in the basement.

I kept my head down trying not to make direct eye contact with the bald, tubby man who by this point was double fisting what appeared to be apple fritters while keeping one eye on us from the kitchen. I used my peripheral vision to observe as many physical details about the place and the people who'd kidnapped us- the sound of their voices. How many of them were in the house. What they were wearing. And then a thought occurred to me that made me feel a little stupid. Were they even Dmitri's real parents? Probably not. And where was Dmitri? I hadn't seen or heard from him since the day I came over here. I thought back about how much I wanted him to like me and about how I would do almost anything to be the one he picked. I had no idea he would betray me like this and I was so mad at putting myself in this situation. I understood that there was no way of me knowing this would happen, but it didn't sting any less.

When I turned my attention back to the girls who were lined up in the hall with me, I noticed that they seemed to be very excited about being let out of the basement. Many of them were in rags, dirt on their faces and hair greasy stuck to their foreheads. It didn't look like they'd had a shower in some time. I was next to use the bathroom when a black-haired girl pushed in front of me. She caught me off guard so I had little time to react before my new friend stood in between us. "You wait your turn, four."

"If I don't go right now, I'm going to pee all over myself." Four crossed her legs together to make her point.

"Too bad. She was next, so move." My friend gave her a look that had Four switch her gaze and move behind me.

She appeared to be the leader of this group. She had the best organizational skills and she was the most alpha compared to the rest of the girls.

"Her name is Four?" I asked.

"Yeah."

"What's your name?" It was a bit impersonal as there were five of us in the bathroom at one time. The other two girls were trying to splash water on their faces and body as some sort of shower. It was incredibly awkward being expected to use the bathroom in front of four other people.

"You can call me Two." She said.

"But what's your real name?" I asked.

"We get in trouble if we use our real names." She held the

toilet paper and handed me a handful of tissue. "You'd better hurry if you gotta go, or else Four's going to take your turn."

I pulled down my pants and sat on the toilet trying to ignore the humiliation of the situation with the justification that we were all in the same boat and most likely none of them cared too much either. "What's the significance of the number two?" I asked.

Two didn't answer right away. She looked up for a moment at nothing in particular before she responded. "I was the second girl they kidnapped."

My heart sank. This poor girl. She'd been here longer than anyone. "Where's One?" I asked.

"She's been gone for a while now. She was a handful. Would never comply with them and fought back every chance she got." She motioned for me to hurry up and finish.

I pulled my pants up and flushed the toilet. "Where did

they take her?"

"How should I know? Now, wait over there until the rest of us are finished." I did as she said thinking about the long term effects this would have on her, and all these girls. I was terrified for my own safety, but I'd just gotten here. I couldn't imagine staying here for several weeks with no idea what would happen to me.

"You'll get your own name soon. They usually issue them after a few days." Four whispered in my ear. "A pretty thing like you will probably be out of here sooner than later."

"What do you mean?" I asked.

She didn't answer but gave me a hateful sarcastic grin. It took me a minute to think of her words before I realized what she meant. Based on what I'd seen, these people had a lot of money and they were highly organized. Terror slowly dawned on me that based on movies and TV shows that I had seen, that was a trafficking operation. That had to be the only explanation why there were only girls in the basement and why the computer monitors had photographs of girls. These people meant to sell all of us as slaves.

My veins iced over. I gasped and had trouble regaining my breath. There was nothing I could do to stop this. It was happening to me and I had no say in anything. I didn't know what to do. There was no one I could call and nobody knew I was here. The balding tubby Russian man was now urging us back down into the basement. As I started to walk past him, he grabbed my arm and shook his head no. He pointed to another room down the hall and motioned for me to head in that direction. I swallowed hard as fear began to choke me. I wasn't sure what was about to happen.

The man who had posed as Dmitri's father got up from the desk and walked up to me. He picked up a tendril of my hair, rubbed it between his fingers, and dropped it. His eyes looked me up and down as if he were eyeing a prime piece of meat. He said something in Russian to the balding tubby man who took me to that room.

Two stepped up to him."Let me stay with her and show her the ropes since she's new. That way she'll be easier to handle."

He looked at her and then looked at me. "Fine. She's your responsibility. But if she gives us any trouble, you share her fate." He turned around and said something in Russian to the bald, tubby guy. They walked into another room.

"What do you mean? Are you helping them?" I was in shock that she could turn on me.

"No, don't be stupid. I'm trying to help you. Now listen, you're going to take a shower and when you get out, I am going to dry your hair. They're going to want you to wear one of their dresses and look nice."

"Why?" I was shaking.

"Because they're going to take several photographs of you. And then they're going to post them on the dark web and start taking bids." Four grabbed me by the shoulders. "Don't give them a problem and you will be safe."

I couldn't speak. It was all too unbelievable to process.

"Hey, did you hear me?" She asked.

I nodded my head in absence of my voice speaking for me.

Four made eye contact with me. "Do you understand what's going on? You're going to be sold to the highest bidder. We all will be."

CHAPTER 7

My mother told me once if I was ever attacked that it was my soul mission to fight with everything I had to get away. Kick, scream, gouge their eyeballs out of their sockets. Whatever I could do to buy a couple of seconds so I could run. She explained that for the most part, attackers didn't want victims who were going to be a problem for them, so they looked for compliant personality types that they thought would do what they were told and not fight back. Part of me felt like I had disappointed her. Had I looked to Dmitri to be a girl who would have easily complied? My heart sank into my stomach. This wasn't my fault, but why did I feel responsible?

Her voice ran through my head on repeat the past four weeks. I looked for an opportunity to run, to redeem myself in my mother's eyes. Every morning they would let us out to relieve ourselves, give us what they considered was breakfast, and then return us to the basement. We only showered once a week in rotation and were given a limited amount of time to do it. The routine ran like clockwork. I realized that was something that worked in my favor. It would be easy to predict their behavior when I knew what to expect. All I had to do was watch them as much as I could when I got the chance. I could study their movements and use it to plan my escape.

Nighttime was an opportunity for all of us to quietly talk about a plan to escape. Most girls were terrified to try to leave, believing they would be severely hurt if they did. All I knew was that if they sold me to someone and I left this house, the chances of my parents or law enforcement finding me would go from bleak to non-existent. I had to find a way to escape before they found a buyer for me. This morning I decided that I'd had enough of it. The fear and apprehension of waiting to find out which one of us was going to be abused next. If we stayed here, we might not ever make it out alive.

I stood in line for the bathroom and watched Dimitri's dad as he sat in front of the computer logging in his password. I'd noticed that the clock on the kitchen wall always said seven o'clock every morning. These people kept a strict schedule. It was the same time we were being given this opportunity to go to the bathroom and get breakfast that the man that I only knew to be Dmitri's father would sit down to his computer screens and log into his computer. Each morning I would watch him enter his password to gain access to his files. It took me a couple of weeks but I believed that I had the password memorized based on the position of his hands.

Typing class was never my favorite but I gave a quick silent prayer to the Lord above for being required to take it in school. Now that I knew his password, I just had to find a way to gain access to his computer. It was important to do this because our shackles were electronically controlled from his computer. There were several times that I witnessed him unlock our shackles when we had to take a shower. If I could gain access, maybe I could unlock all the girls' shackles and we could find a way to escape. Maybe since there were more of us than them, we could overpower them.

This morning as we're going to the bathroom and getting our food, I noticed that he got up from the computer and went into the other room. "Let me know if he comes back," I told Two.

"What are you doing? Do you want to get us all in trouble?" She tried to grab my hand but I slipped out of her grip and headed toward the computer.

I sat at the computer and moved the mouse so that it would bring me to the login screen. I looked behind me to make sure he wasn't coming back and then punched in a series of letters and numbers. I hit the enter key but nothing happened. I must have punched it in wrong. Again, I looked behind my shoulder making sure that nobody was coming to get me. I could feel that I only had a few seconds left. As I typed the password a second time, the screen turned green and gave me access. That's when I felt a cold hand on my shoulder and a sharp Russian tongue cursing at me. He grabbed me by the arm and yanked me out of the chair onto the ground. I put up my hands in an effort to protect my body, but he picked me up and threw me down again in the direction of the basement. "You want to be difficult, eh? Then you're going to feel what it's like when you're difficult." His thick Russian accent fought for control over his words. "Ariel, take her to the basement and chain her to the wall."

"No, please. I'm sorry. It won't happen again. I'll be good, I promise!" I cried.

"Too late for that. Lucky for you, I've got a buyer. One that wants his girls to be nice and pretty. Otherwise, I might have rearranged your face. But no matter, you won't be my problem for much longer."

I don't know what got into me, but my tears stopped and the fear that I'd been under for four weeks transformed into rage. Suddenly I didn't care what he could do to me. As his flunky held me up, I spit in his face. He touched his hand to his cheek and wiped my spit off then slapped me across the curve of my jaw. Ariel pushed me into the basement and shut the door.

I tasted the metallic flavor of blood and held my cheek. I was so close. I could have gotten myself and the other girls out if I had only had another couple of seconds.

"What are you doing? Are you trying to get all of us killed?" Two yelled.

I didn't answer her and instead slid down the wall hugging my knees to my chest and wondering if I would ever see my mother again.

CHAPTER 8

Most of the girls weren't talking to me. They thought my escape attempt was foolish and put all their lives in danger. Others understood what I was trying to do. I couldn't understand why they were all just letting this happen. It didn't make any sense.

I found a wooden crate under the stairs, brought it out in the middle of the basement, turned it over, and stepped on it. "Excuse me, I want to say something."

The girls stopped what they were doing and looked at me. "Why don't you keep your voice down?" Two responded.

"What's your problem? Why aren't you fighting harder? Don't you want to get out of this place?" Frustrated tears filled my eyes as I looked around the room.

"We're all trying to survive, twenty-six. But we know we could die if we resist. Why don't you get a clue?" Two said.

"They're going to sell us. All of us. And if you leave here, the chance that you will be found alive somewhere in the world is slim to none." I looked at Two. "And my name is not Twenty-six. It's Marlene and I'm not playing their game anymore."

Our conversation was interrupted by the door opening. Ariel came downstairs and looked at us. He pointed to me and then pointed upstairs. I froze afraid of what was about to come next. I watched the girls' expression as I moved toward the stairs. Some had concern for me and others had fear in their eyes mixed with relief that it wasn't them. I didn't hold it against them though. I understood the strain and pressure we were all under. The truth was that I couldn't expect them to react the way I wanted them to or in accordance with the way I thought the world should work. There weren't any rules in a situation like this. I'd have to figure it out for myself and then hopefully save them too.

He led me to the bathroom and motioned for me to take a shower and get dressed. "No," I said.

Dmitri's father came in. "You will do as you are told. You

have a new master coming today and unless you want to leave here in trash bags, you'd better do as you are told."

He closed the distance between us staring into my eyes but more so into my soul. He grabbed the shackles between my wrists and dragged me over to the computer. Then he typed on the keyboard, I presumed he was typing in the code to unlock my shackles so I could take a shower. "Go get ready and don't give us any trouble."

I shut the bathroom door behind me and sat down on the floor. I wasn't sure how to handle this or what to do. If I didn't comply I could get seriously hurt, or worse. If I did comply, I may never see my parents again. This way, if I did go with them, there would be a small window of opportunity to escape. And all I needed was just a tiny window of opportunity. At least, just long enough to inform the sheriff's office so they could save the others.

Speaking of windows, there wasn't one, so making my escape wasn't going to happen here. I showered quickly and dried off, put on a red dress that was already hanging up in the bathroom. I walked out into the living room to see two men in black jackets standing there. They were talking about picking up the package which I assumed meant me.

"Be careful with her, she's a feisty one." Dmitri's father said.

"Don't talk about me like that." I forced myself to find the courage to speak up.

"You will go with these men without trouble, understand?" His eyes seem to sparkle.

I watched the two men pass a suitcase over to him. He opened it to reveal stacks of cash in bundles.

"Pleasure doing business with you gentlemen. She's all yours." He gave a wide perverse grin that sent adrenaline through my body..

As soon as we walked out of the house my eyes adjusted. I saw the street and grass and cars and it almost brought tears to my eyes. It had been so long since I'd seen daylight in a neighborhood. A voice inside my head screamed at me that this was my chance. I had to think quickly and figure out a plan.

We were almost in the car and I knew that if I got into that car I may never have another chance to get away. So I kicked one of the guys hard in the knee. He collapsed and ran out into the road and across the street. The other guy chased after me. I screamed for anyone to help me but saw no one out in the street. He chased me as I ran into another person's yard, grabbed my foot, and tripped me. We both went tumbling to the ground.

"So that's what he meant by feisty, huh?" He said.

The other guy caught up to us, limping as he walked and they both grabbed me and carried me back to the black van. I kicked and screamed until they lost their grip on me. I was able to break away from one of them but the other one still had a firm grip on my arm. The first man was able to recover his grip on me and together they threw me into the van as I screamed and fought the entire time. I punched and slapped at both of them until I felt a prick in my shoulder. I'd been stuck with something. My head began to swoon and I had trouble concentrating. I heard them talk about where they were going as my eyes shut and my brain drifted off into the sleepy blackness of the unknown.

CHAPTER 9

Various noises in my ears started out far away and then got louder. My eyes slowly opened as my head tried to clear the space from the fogginess. It took a minute before I realized that my body couldn't move freely. I was disoriented and unsure of what was happening. Instinctively, I curled my body into the fetal position to protect myself. A groan escaped my lips.

The pulsing rhythm of the tires vibrated beneath me. Panic set in and I recalled what had happened to land me in the back of the van. I lifted my head to see who was in the front seat but all I could see were two men dressed in black wearing baseball hats. It was difficult to make out their faces. I said nothing, hoping it wasn't too late to pretend I was still asleep. I didn't want them to know I was awake.

The metal frame I was laying on poked me in the back causing an uncomfortable pain. I was afraid to move and tried to stay still. Thoughts were flashing in my head and I tried to mentally grab one that would help me figure out how to get out of this mess. I kept looking at the front of the van to watch the men. They were talking to each other. I wasn't sure what they were saying because the radio was kinda loud. My brain tried to memorize the driver's facial features. If I could remember as many details as possible, maybe it would help later when I got away. I laid my head back down on the metal floor of the van and squeezed my eyes shut. This wasn't real. It couldn't be real. I gave a silent prayer to God that he would help me out of this nightmare.

I heard the sound of the radio increase and a man's voice filled the cab of the van. I opened my eyes slowly and listened carefully to what the voice was saying.

"...police and volunteers have formed a search party for Marlene Smith, a Bradford High School senior who went missing four weeks ago after leaving school..."

Hearing my name on the radio spiked the adrenaline response in my body and sent a surge of it to my heart. My breath caught in my throat and a tiny light of hope burned inside of me. Had they really been looking for me all this time? A wide grin formed on my face and with it a waterfall of tears. I stayed very still so as not to tip off either of the men that I was awake.

I wasn't sure I heard correctly at first. The announcer said my name so quickly that I almost didn't catch it until he continued to talk about the search. Part of me didn't want to believe the news. I didn't want to get my hopes up.

I squeezed my fists in excitement. It was the only physical way to express my excitement without drawing attention to myself. Searching my mind for an idea- any idea- that would give me a plan to escape.

The announcer said my name again as he was reporting the rest of the story and there was now no doubt. My mother and father were looking for me! For the first time in over a month, I felt like I had a real shot at being rescued. But I couldn't wait on the police or my parents. I had to figure out a way to get away from these men before we reached the location they were taking me to. I swallowed hard as my body was stiff and aching.

Slowly, I brought my hands up to my face so I could see what kind of restraint they had me in. It was a zip tie handcuff. My wrists were red and cut in some areas from the thick plastic. I used my teeth to try to bite through the plastic but it was too thick.

The man in black sitting in the passenger seat turned around just as I was trying to bite through my constraints. "She's trying to get out!" He unbuckled his seatbelt and tried to get to the back of the van.

He was a huge fat guy and the mere size of his silhouette coming toward me freaked me out. There was nothing I could do. I put my hands and legs up to protect my body. "What are you doing awake." The man snarled at me.

"You know what to do." The driver yelled back to the big guy.

I wrestled with the man trying to keep him away from me by kicking. I screamed wildly. My plan was to keep him from hurting me and maybe get a few jabs in myself. Knowing that people were out looking for me renewed my strength. I was not going to go down without a fight. He pinned me down and leaned on my back.

"Get off of me!" I screamed.

I struggled underneath his body weight. He ignored me and pulled something out from his pocket. I feared it was a knife or a gun. Was he going to shoot me now? I tried to inhale and scream again but he leaned on me harder preventing me from deeply inhaling. Panic set in as I couldn't get a good breath so I wiggled my body to try to get out from underneath him. "I can't breathe! Please get off me!" I pleaded.

My legs were burning and tiring out. At this rate, I would lose energy if I continued to fight against him.

But I couldn't give up now. I had to stay awake. My life depended on keeping my wits about me. I stopped kicking hoping he would get off of me at least long enough for me to catch my breath. "Stop fighting." The man said.

My arms and legs felt like heavyweights. He took a second focused on something in his hands. Disappointment in the form of tears filled my eyes. I was so exhausted that all I could do was just lay there. I tried moving my hands up to my face but he felt me move and pressed his body weight into me to keep me still. "Be still. Don't move again, do you hear me?" He threatened.

I nodded my head in compliance.

"Pull over, Hank." He called to the front of the van.

The driver let out a stream of curses. Hank. His name was Hank. I had to remember that. This guy had messed up now.

"Why did you say my name?" Hank yelled. "You idiot!"

The two exchanged curse-laden insults back and forth and for a moment I thought I'd be able to wiggle out from under him. "I can't pull over. Give her another dose!"

The man leaning on me turned his attention back to what he was doing. I shot him a dirty look. When I had regained some of my energy, I would try to resist him. That's when I saw him with the syringe in his hand.

A renewed surge of adrenaline shot through me again and I managed to knock the syringe out of his hand. I couldn't lose consciousness again. My hands, although tied together, I tried to swing at him. He blocked me with his arm and slapped me. I fell to the floor of the van as the aftershock of the slap shook my jaw.

"This only ends badly for you, girl. I'm not going to tell you again."

He yanked my arm closer to him, picked up the syringe, and stuck it in my arm. I jerked loose from him and began to punch his chest with my balled up fists. He grabbed my hands and held them. "You'll calm down in a minute." He said.

Forced to be still, I started to notice that my eyelids were growing heavy and my vision was blurred. Fear gripped me as I knew I was losing this fight. I tried to fight it with all that I had. "You'll never get away with this," I threatened.

"You're hardly the first job we've had, darling." He laughed. "And you won't be the last."

My arms felt like rubber bands. I could no longer fight him off and laid there still. My mind felt like it was entering a dark abyss. The harder I tried to fight walking into the darkness, the less control I had over it. It was frightening to lose control and even more terrifying was to not know when or if I would ever wake up again. I tried to pull my hands up to my chest and return to the fetal position and felt the man finally take his weight off of me. I heard whimpers and realized the sound was mine.

CHAPTER 10

I didn't know if it was the faint voices I heard or the realization that the rhythm of the drive had stopped that led me to wake up. I had a raging headache. My hand instinctively reached for my head but because my wrists were tied, I ended up using both of them to hold my head. There was a noise outside of the van and I also smelled gasoline. I sat up to look at the front of the van to see if either of the men were inside but they weren't. They must be getting gas.

There were three voices speaking outside of the van. One was unrecognizable, but the other two I identified as the two men who had kidnapped me. Quietly, I tried to move but I couldn't. I looked down and realized that I had a pair of zip ties and duct tape wrapped around my feet. My knees were locked together and I couldn't move. There was no obvious answer as to why my mouth wasn't covered but I was grateful for the break. I took a deep breath and let out the biggest blood curdling scream that I've ever attempted.

When I stopped, I heard a commotion like feet shuffling running toward the van. Then I heard the unrecognizable voice speak, "Who's in there?"

There was a pause before I heard one of the kidnappers respond. "Oh, that's just my niece playing a prank. She thinks it's funny to pretend that she's been kidnapped. Especially when we drive my van."

The other kidnapper laughed slightly and I could only assume it was to help sell the lie.

I screamed again. "Please help me, I've been kidnapped!"

"That doesn't sound like a prank to me. Open the door!" The stranger shouted.

The next sound I heard was a couple of bumps against the van as if a large object had been thrown against it. Sweat formed on my forehead as I tried to hear what was going on outside of the van. My throat was sore from screaming so much, but I couldn't waste this chance to be rescued.

Somebody had to hear me.

"They're going to kill me, please help me!" My body shook violently but there was nothing I could do to calm myself. I was too close to freedom to be afraid any longer.

The handle on the back of the van door clicked and then opened, letting the lights from the convenience store parking lot shine in. I squinted as my eyes tried to adjust. Standing there was a shorter guy with sandy blonde hair and a mustache. When he saw me his eyes widened in surprise.

"Please help me." I begged.

He opened his mouth to utter a word but was abruptly silenced by a wire cord around his neck. The driver had removed it from his pocket. He tightened it around the good samaritan's neck, pulling from both sides. The stranger brought both hands up to his neck instinctively and clawed at the wire cord. It was too tight for him to get a grip on it.

I was helpless to do anything but lay there and watch this terror unfold in front of me.

"You wanna be a big man? You wanna get involved?" The driver taunted. "Well, this is what butting into other people's business gets ya."

My heart pounded in my chest as tears streamed down my face. I could see it in his eyes the moment of realization that he would never get out of this. He still fought valiantly trying to grab at the driver who was behind him. I was no use. His eyes fluttered followed by a few gurgling noises and then his body went limp. The pupils of his eyes glazed over into a haunting stare and I knew I was no longer looking at a man with a soul, but a hollow empty shell.

My body wouldn't stop shaking. The horror of what I just witnessed wouldn't shake loose from my brain. Both men worked quickly and grabbed the guy by his head and legs, pushing him into the back of the van and laying him next to me before shutting the door. I looked at his lifeless body still fresh from the kill and leaned over to throw up. I was so hot and sweaty I could feel myself about to pass out. I couldn't remember anything after that.

CHAPTER 11

A single drop of sweat dripped down the bridge of my nose. Noticeably the climate changed and it was uncomfortably hot.

"Not much longer now." The driver reached down to scratch his leg and let out a loud belch.

"Did you confirm with our contact that we were en route with the package?" The man sitting in the passenger's seat asked.

"I was waiting until we got into Mexico."

So that's where they were taking me. I strained to listen further.

"What was up with killing that guy?" The passenger accused.

"What else did you expect me to do?" The driver replied. " The both of them were making so much noise they were gonna attract attention."

"I'm just saying- now we gotta find a place to bury the body. It's more work, is all." The passenger said.

I stayed frozen for another hour trying not to freak out about the dead man lying next to me. His eyes were slightly open and appeared to stare straight into my soul. There was also a disgusting smell and I surmised that the heat was starting to decompose the body. I tried holding my breath but every time I had to release it, I'd just inhale a deep breath of this foul stench.

A familiar chime rang on a cell phone indicating that one of the men was getting an incoming video call. I heard rustling as if they were trying to grab their phones out of their pockets to determine which phone was ringing. There were a few seconds of silence and then a familiar voice was on the other end. I couldn't quite place it as it was hard to hear, but I knew that I had heard that voice at some time not too long ago.

Gambling that they were too preoccupied with this video call to notice me, I raised my head slightly to try to get a look at who was on the other end of the phone. Unfortunately, I couldn't see anything

"You have the package?" the voice said.

"Yeah, boss. We're headed for the border now." The passenger sounded eager like he wanted to please this guy.

"Any problems?" The voice asked.

The two men looked at each other before the driver spoke for both of them. "Just a minor one, but we took care of it."

There was a pause. "Don't be late." The video chat bell rang signaling that the voice had hung up the call.

I couldn't figure out where I'd heard that voice before. It was so familiar yet I couldn't place it.

The driver turned left causing the dead body to shift closer toward me. I held back the vomit that was rising in my throat. The van stopped. My heart was in my throat competing with the vomit to choke me. I peeked and saw the two men get out of the van. I struggled to prop my body against the back door so I could get a look out of the window. There were a group of men talking to the two men who had kidnapped me. They had tattoos on their face and body and many of them had a matching tattoo insignia. I assumed those were gang tattoos. Terrified they'd see me, I tried to duck down while still peeking.

The driver spoke to one man who was standing in front of all the other men. He yelled at the leader in Spanish. They had an exchange of words and then out of nowhere the leader of the gang pulled out a gun and shot the driver. I saw the passenger jump back in shock. His tone of voice also changed. He waved his arms in the air and it sounded like he was begging the man not to kill him, too. The gang leader looked at him for a moment before raising his gun and shooting him dead where he stood.

I covered my mouth to prevent myself from screaming. Out of nowhere, I heard other shots ring out. The gang members appeared surprised and they all turned around to find a group of men shooting at them. I watched them take cover and start shooting back. What was going on? Did I really end up in the middle of a gang war in Mexico?

I dove to the floor and covered my head praying that no stray bullets would pierce the metal van and hit me.

Sirens blasted in the air getting louder as the shooting died down. For several long minutes, I heard nothing. Then I heard a voice speak English. "Check the van!"

Terror swept through me like a tornado. I couldn't move

83

myself to move. The sound of footsteps got closer. This was it. I was going to die right here. I closed my eyes and said a prayer to God to keep my parents safe.

I heard the back door of the van open and a black-haired man stood there in a blazer and blue jeans staring back at me. On his blazer jacket, he wore a metal badge. My brain slowly realized he was a police officer. "Marlene? Is that your name?" He asked.

Too overwhelmed, I nodded my head and began to cry.

The cop held out of hand for me to help me out of the van. I pulled him in tight to me and didn't want to let him go. He was the first figure of normalcy I had seen in a month.

"Are you hurt?" He asked.

Still sobbing I mustered up the strength to answer. "No."

"You are safe." He placed a hand on my shoulder to comfort me. "Stay here. I have an ambulance on the way."

"Thank you," I muttered.

I sat on the ground watching the police work the crime scene when I noticed a cop around the bodies of the driver and passenger. He was digging in their pockets. He pulled out a cell phone from the driver's pocket and put it in his own. I couldn't help think the phone was evidence and it was strange that they were handling it without gloves. I dismissed the thought, grateful to finally be safe. I was finally free.

CHAPTER 12

A week later I was still in the hospital for dehydration and malnourishment among a couple of other things. My mother never left my side. My father still had to work but would come to the hospital every day after work and sit with me while my mother got some sleep. I told them everything and apologized for disobeying them that day and sneaking over to Dmitri's house.

FBI Special Agent Don Roberts was the man who pulled me out of the van that day. He came by to check on me and to get my account of the events. I told him everything. About Dmitri and his parents. About the other girls locked in the basement. About the two guys who drove me to Mexico and the poor unfortunate stranger who died trying to help me.

Special Agent Roberts looked at me strangely. "This isn't adding up, Marlene."

"What do you mean?" I asked.

He took a long pause. "We can confirm there was a student named Dmitri who attended your school, but we cannot confirm that his parents worked at the embassy. He has since withdrawn from high school and we are checking into that."

"All I know is what he told me," I was shocked.

"There's something else," he began. "We went to the house you described.

"Were you able to save the women?" I was excited that all those girls would be saved.

"There were no women. There was no sign of anyone in the basement or in the house. According to the real estate company, that house has been vacant for months."

The news hit me right in the gut and blasted the air right out of my lungs. "What do you mean? I spent a month locked up in that basement with them."

"Our team went through the entire house and did not find one clue that could determine that anyone you describe ever lived there."

CHAPTER 13

I'd been at this for hours and I was still getting the same results. This couldn't be a coincidence. Not after everything I'd been through. My posts on Facebook and Instagram about the kidnapping and my story had been wiped clean from the internet saying that it violated their terms of service. I knew that I hadn't violated any rules. This was something else. Something more devious. I tried it several times and each time I refreshed the page it came up blank.

"Mom!" I shouted down the hall until she answered me. "Please come here!" I pounded my finger on the keyboard, hitting the 'enter' key repeatedly until my finger turned red and throbbed.

"What is it, sweetheart? What's wrong?" My mom peered into my room looking concerned.

"Look at this," I explained and showed her what I was talking about. "You can't tell me this is some coincidence."

"That doesn't seem so strange to me, darling." My mother insisted. "I mean if you've told your story and they pulled it down, then maybe it's too intense for the internet."

"Something is going on, mom. I'm not imagining it." I turned to her, my cheeks burned in anger and frustration.

"Calm down, honey. It will all be alright." She shifted her stance to stand in front of me. "Maybe if you step away from the computer for awhile. It's making you a little paranoid."

"I'm not crazy, mom. Don't call me crazy!" Tears streamed

down my face. I was so hurt that she could call me paranoid.

"I didn't call you crazy, Marlene. Please calm down." She gave me a strange look.

I blurted out. "You and dad can't pretend it didn't happen! It happened. It happened to me!"

I began crying and shaking, unsure of what I was going to do. The room felt heavy and dark. I tried taking a deep breath in but the air seemed too thick.

My mom opened her arms and stepped forward to embrace me, "We know it happened, Marlene. We are so sorry it happened to you."

She held me in her arms and for a moment I felt like that little girl who scraped her knee and was healed by her mother's love. "Just believe me," I pleaded.

"I do believe you." She cried.

"They're coming after me. It's not over." I released myself

from her embrace and ran out of my room, down the stairs, and bumped into my father.

"What's going on, pumpkin?" He grabbed my shoulders.

"They're going to come after me, daddy. I need you to believe me. Please daddy!" I cried.

"You've been through a traumatic time, Marlene. Calm down." He said.

"They're taking my posts down on social media. They don't want the truth out there." I plead.

"Who's taking your posts down?" He looked at me sideways. "Who are you talking about?"

"The people who kidnapped me. They had a whole system set up. They know how to hack into any system, I'm sure of it." I heaved in a bunch of air through my mouth as my nose was stuffed up with mucus. I leaned my head into my father's chest.

"The kidnappers are dead, Marlene. Don't you remember

what happened in Mexico?" My dad put his hand on my head.

"No! Those were the guys who were going to deliver me to the guy who paid for me. They weren't the masterminds behind this. Please daddy, believe me."

"I do believe you, princess." He said. "But you have to calm down. It won't resolve anything by dwelling on it. You're scaring us Marlene."

His comment infuriated me. I pulled away from him. "I have a right to dwell on it daddy." I lifted my arms and mimicked air quotes on the word 'dwell' in a condescending tone. "You and mom don't understand. Nobody understands." I pushed past him and ran out the door before either one of them could stop me.

I took off running in the direction of Dmitri's house. It was the one place that could prove my story true. I pumped my hands and let my feet carry me a couple blocks until I was in front of his house. I bent over in his driveway, trying to get my breath. I heard there were new owners but I didn't care. For all I knew, they could have been in on it, too.

Two kids from the neighborhood rode past me on their bikes, reminding me that before all of this life was simpler and I wished I still felt that way. I wished I could have gone back before all of this. I felt so ashamed of having chased Dmitri, lying to my parents and sneaking over to his house.

I walked up to the house and knocked on the door. A woman with short black hair and small frame answered the door wiping her hands with a dishcloth. "Can I help you?"

"I'm sorry, ma'am." I pushed past her and ran inside, ignoring her screams and protests.

"Tom! Help!" She called for a man named Tom, who I assumed was her husband.

He followed me into the kitchen. "Who are you? What are you doing in our home?" The man screamed.

I noticed the house was furnished differently this time than from what I remembered. I opened the basement door.

"Hillary, call the police!"

I turned on the basement light and ran down the stairs. My heartbeat violently as I looked around. A shock of disbelief came over me. No one was there. Not one person was down in that basement. This couldn't be reality. The walls were painted white and drywall covered the wood slats that were there before.

I fell to my knees in utter desperation. I knew I wasn't imagining all of this but it was all too overwhelming. Pulling my knees into my chest, I began crying. A voice peered from out of the confusion repeating the words, "I'm not crazy. I'm not crazy. I'm not crazy." That's when I realized the voice I heard was my own.

Dropping my head in my hands, I rocked back and forth unable to stop the panicked feeling swelling up inside of me. A barrage of footsteps stomped down the stairs and then I felt several pairs of hands grab my arms. Officers held me down as I screamed. They fastened tight handcuffs around my wrists.

I'm not crazy. I know I'm not crazy. They were here. It happened to me.

CHAPTER 14

"Marlene, would you like to speak to the group today?" Mrs. Anderson asked. She was the psych ward counselor and had been my one-on-one therapist for the past four days.

I looked around to see everyone in the group looking at me. My palms began to sweat as I shook my head no. The room was filled with about twelve other residents here all dealing with their own mental health issues. Some seemed crazy while others seemed stressed but normal. I didn't belong here and would probably never forgive my parents for admitting me.

"This concludes our meeting for today," Mrs. Anderson dismissed us. I returned to my room and laid down on the bed, ignoring my roommate's failed attempts at singing to an old eighties song.

There was a knock on our open door. One of the staff called out to me. "Marlene, don't forget you have a session in about five minutes." She smiled and then left.

Early on in my stay here I tried to tell the staff about my story. I tried to give them the information about the kidnappers and Dmitri and his parents, but everyone looked at me like I had lost my mind. They all had the same fake smile plastered on their faces, head cocked to the side, nodding in understanding, but I could tell they didn't believe me. They thought I was just another crazy person telling made up stories.

I got up and walked down the hall to Mrs. Anderson's office, knocked on her door, and waited for her to answer. She opened the door. "Come in, please." She gestured for me to sit in a chair on the opposite side of hers across from her desk.

Mrs. Anderson was smart and appeared to be a decent human being to me, but I felt like she was just patronizing me at times. I was so exhausted from this week and trying to convince everybody that my story was true. Eventually, I gave up trying.

I grabbed the water bottle sitting next to my chair, unscrewed the cap and took a big swig.

"You have done well these past four days." She tapped her pen on the desk. "You will be able to go home tomorrow."

A sliver of a smile appeared out of the corner of my mouth. It had been the first smile in over a week. What did it mean that I could go home? I'd go back into my parent's house where neither of them believed me. I sunk lower in my chair and stared out of the window watching a bird take flight. I wished I could have been a bird and flown far away from my life here.

"Do you want to add anything to our conversation yesterday?" She asked.

"No, ma'am." I'd already told her everything that happened to me. It felt like wasted effort to try and convince the people around me that I was still in danger.

"What about your social media posts. Why do you think there are people who are blocking your posts?" She asked.

"Because I can identify them. I've seen their faces and I know who they are. I can point them out if I had to, but you don't believe me. Nobody does." Sitting in the leather chair, I drew my knees up into my chest.

"And why do you think they would risk coming after you?" She asked.

"Because they probably know about what happened to the two guys who were taking me to Mexico. They know by now that they were killed and that I was set free. It was all over the news." I answered.

The press had been camped outside my house for days trying to get an interview with me. My father's attorney managed to arrange security to protect me from it. A pang of guilt and shame overwhelmed me. I'd put my parents through so much worry. All I wanted was to get out of here and return to some kind of normal life. Although I knew my life would never be normal again. This wasn't the kind of thing you just moved on from.

I missed my friends and I missed high school. I just wanted to put the whole thing behind me. It still stung that no one believed me. I didn't know what I was going to do when I left. I still had to protect myself because I knew it wasn't over. There's no way they'd let me live having witnessed what I saw.

My heart was having trouble forgiving my parents. They were the ones who admitted me into this program. I'd been so angry with them four days ago, resolving never to forgive them. My mother was crying when they took me away. My father assured me everything would be alright. But to me? It was a betrayal. Why didn't they just believe me? Especially after what I'd just been through. How could they do this to me?

Feelings of bitterness swelled inside of me. I wiped the tears away from my eyes, pretending there was something caught in them.

"You're going to be okay." Mrs. Anderson said.

"How do you know?" I turned my head to wait for her response.

"Because you're a survivor." She retorted. "And that's evidenced by the fact you're still sitting here today."

It was a kind compliment and part of me knew it was the truth, but I felt so alone. Nobody understood what I'd gone through. And I felt guilt for all those women who didn't get away. The women who would still have to suffer through the filthy conditions of a basement, and the humiliation of being sold as an object to the highest bidder. I wondered where they were right now.

My eyes shifted back to the birds outside wishing again that I could be one of them and fly north for the winter. Maybe I could change my name, dye my hair and be somebody entirely different.

"Was there anything else you wanted to discuss today, Marlene?" Mrs. Anderson asked.

"No," I said.

"Okay then. I'll sign your discharge papers today. Your parents will be here tomorrow to pick you up." She shuffled the papers on her desk.

"Thank you for being so kind to me," I said.

"It's been a pleasure to work with you, Marlene. Remember the tools you learned here when things get scary." She stood up and walked around the table to shake my hand. I reached out to meet her halfway and she held my hand for a moment. "I know it might be difficult to understand or believe right now, but you have parents who love you and who are on your side. Reach out to them when you start feeling anxious."

"I'll try to remember that," I said.

She opened the door to her office. I stood up and gave her a hug. "Thank you."

She gave me an encouraging smile.

I went back to my room and laid on the bed I'd made up that morning. We were responsible for making our beds each morning. It was one of the rules and honestly, kind of a confidence builder for me. It was something I could accomplish each day and feel good about.

I put my hands behind my head and crossed my ankles wondering when the terror in my mind would stop and when I would return to that naive seventeen year old girl again, knowing full well that girl was dead.

CHAPTER 15

I dragged my feet as I slogged down the hallway on my first day back to school. I could feel the eyeballs of every person on me as I passed them. They knew what happened to me because every news and media channel had been covering it over the past week. I was way past self-conscious and was questioning whether returning to school this soon was a good idea.

Even Monica and Lucy had very little to say and I assumed it was because they didn't know what to say. There wasn't much one could say to a friend who had just returned from spending almost two months kidnapped and recovering. Janis hadn't shown her face or caused problems either, which was extraordinary- for her.

I found myself in Mrs. Schroeder's Social Science class and plopped myself in my old seat. Usually I'd wear my hair in a ponytail, but today I wore it down. In my mind, it protected me, like a socially acceptable wall around my eyes. I was half-heartedly paying attention, instead of doodling in my notebook. The lights dimmed and I looked up to see that she was showing some kind of video clip. I returned to my doodles and the internal spaces in my mind where I felt safe.

"The President and I have discussed this in detail and I can assure you that nothing is more important to him than securing our borders..."

I looked up and on the screen at the man who was the face of the voice I heard in the van.

"That's George L. Hullman, Homeland Security Advisor to the President speaking about the meeting he had yesterday with...." the news announcer said.

George L. Hullman. Security Advisor to the President.

My knees began to shake and my heart pounded. This was the man who had paid for me from the Russian couple. If that was true, then I wasn't crazy. There was something big going on and I was right at the center of it.

Paranoid, I looked around at my classmates. I envied how carefree they were. They knew nothing about the evil and darkness outside of these walls.

I wasn't sure what I should do. If someone this high up to the president was involved in human trafficking, then anything was possible. Did the president know?

That meant I wasn't safe. Not at home and not here at school.

"Excuse me, Mrs. Schroeder. May I please use the restroom?" I asked.

She nodded. I grabbed my backpack and headed out of the door toward the school exit. My parents would know what to do. I just had to get home and explain what I saw. Then they would call Special Agent Roberts and he would take it from there. Except that-- he was part of the FBI-- that meant he was employed by the same organization that was under the president. What if he was in on all of this too? My memory flashed back to the day I was rescued when I noticed one of the agents grab the phone out of the kidnapper's pocket and put it in his own. Could he have been part of all of this too?

As I flung open the door and ran down the steps, I was confronted by a black sedan that pulled up onto the sidewalk, blocking my path.

The window rolled down to reveal a man in a black leather jacket with black hair and a goatee. He pulled out a pistol and showed it to me. "Marlene. Nice to see you again."

I started to walk backward but he lifted the pistol into plain view reminding me not to move.

"Listen, don't get any ideas about talking to that FBI pal of yours. We're watching you. This ain't over."

He sped away as fast as he had arrived. I stood there shaking and frozen. I didn't know what to do. I thought the nightmare had ended, but it hadn't.

It was just the beginning.

Part II

CHAPTER 16

I watched as the black sedan drove away, its red lights glowing as it rounded the corner moving away from my school's parking lot. The FBI agents inside on their way back to headquarters, leaving me terrified and more confused. The surreal reality hit me and I couldn't believe that I was in the middle of something that felt like a movie. Except that I wasn't an actor and didn't go home to my safe life after the director called cut.

My knees weakened as I stood there alone, looking down the street where the sedan used to be. What if I was being watched? I knew I might not be safe and needed to surround myself with other people. I turned around and walked back into the school, down the hall, and opened the door to my classroom. Everyone looked at me. First, because I interrupted the lesson and then a familiar facial expression spread across all their faces. They recognized me, but not just as Marlene, the happy-go-lucky girl. That person no longer existed to them. Now I was the girl who got kidnapped. The looks of pity and scrutiny were nearly overwhelming. They all knew what happened to me. It had been all over the news. They also knew that I had been institutionalized, which made it harder to live down the stigma that I was insane.

I sulked down in my chair, counting down the minutes until class was over and I could go to lunch. Finally, the bell rang, and I raced out of the classroom, trying to catch my breath from the claustrophobic pressure building on me. The cafeteria was full of students, including my friends. It was the last place I wanted to sit down and eat. All those eyes burrowing into my skin, judging me. Or worse, feeling sorry for me. I decided to go to the library instead. I opened the door and saw that there weren't many students in there.

"Hi Marlene," Mrs. Thompson greeted. She was the school's librarian and had always been kind to me. "Not hungry today?"

"No, ma'am. Besides, it's just a little too busy in the cafeteria. Would it be alright if ate my lunch in here?" I asked.

Mrs. Thompson pushed her glasses up the bridge of her nose and gave me a gentle smile. "Of course. Just don't tell anyone that I've gone soft." She smiled.

It was a pleasant change of pace to be treated and joked around with, like everything was normal. Mrs. Thompson most likely knew what had happened to me, but she was gracious enough not to act like she did. I snickered, and it was the first time I'd genuinely wanted to do so. I sat down and unwrapped the sandwich my mom had packed for me. I pulled out the accompanying snacks and glanced at the glass doors of the library. Janice walked by just at that moment and looked in. She saw me, and her facial expression morphed into a weird combination of sorrow and anger. She stopped and just stood there. It was too late for me to pretend not to notice her, and so I stared back. It felt like forever, but finally I saw the corner of her mouth raise in a sympathetic smile and she walked away.

After lunch, I made my way to my next class. The heavy weight of the wood door fought me as I opened it. Thoughts had been racing through my mind all day and the eyes of everyone around me were making me paranoid. There wasn't any place I could be alone without eyeballs boring into me. I thought getting back to school would comfort me, but all it managed to do was make things worse. I suppressed my fear and kept my head high. I couldn't let anything or anyone get to me. There was something very particular I had to accomplish, and I needed to stay strong to do it.

Once home, I closed my front door and locked it before

exhaling deeply. I threw my backpack on the table and rushed upstairs, where I found my laptop on my desk. Opening it, I logged in quickly and typed in the name of the secretary of Homeland Security. There was article after article, and my anxiety rose in my throat. I clicked on a YouTube video and watched him deliver a speech about tolerance and defense of our great nation. His words made me sick. The disgusting hypocrisy I was witnessing enraged me. The tone of his voice differed from the voice I heard on the phone when he was bargaining to buy me. My body stiffened and chills spread down my spine recalling the way he flippantly talked about me. I could feel the bile rise in my throat

I looked up at the clock and realized that it was midnight. Nine hours had passed without me noticing. I stood up and stretched my back and legs, walking around my room. There was a knock at the door.

"Marlene honey. Can I come in?" My mother's voice was on the other side of my bedroom door.

"Yeah, I guess." I said.

She opened the door and peeked her face in. "I don't want to bother you, sweety, but you have eaten nothing or come downstairs. Your father and I were beginning to worry about you. How was your day at school?"

"It was fine." I said flatly.

She hesitated. "Aren't you hungry? I made lasagna for dinner. Would you like me to bring you up a plate?"

The thought of food made me want to throw up. "No...thanks."

I didn't turn around. There was a pause, and a moment later, I heard my door quietly shut. Part of me felt guilty. I knew my mother was trying to help. I understood she probably felt helpless, but I didn't want pity. I wanted justice. And I was going to get it even if I had to scorch every inch of earth between here and D.C. I was going to make Secretary Anderson pay for everything he did to me and those girls locked in the basement. I felt the anger renewed inside of me. At this point I didn't have a plan, but if there was no telling how many other top officials were involved too. I still remembered the horror of being locked up for a month in the basement. The filth and the depravity of all those girls.

And now I had to worry about the FBI causing more problems for me. That's why I was keeping my encounters with them a secret. I didn't want word getting around that I was cooperating with them. I knew that if anyone found out, I would be in real danger. Although, there was no telling who was still watching me. Did the Secretary have his people secretly following me? I started to sound in my head like what I was afraid everyone else was saying behind my back - that I was crazy.

I reasoned that the best thing I could do would be to act like nothing happened. Not only did it seem to make everyone else around me feel normal, but it might save me from anyone trying to kidnap me again. Panic swept over me at the thought. Is everything over? Or is it only the beginning? I never asked for any of this. But I'm going to finish it.

In the midst of this mess, my parents thought it best to send my brother back to school. It was just as well. I knew he felt awkward about the whole situation and didn't know how to talk to me. Everyone around me was acting similarly. Wanting to say something but then thinking better of it. Of course, that makes it even more awkward. It felt like they pitied me. I hated that feeling.

There was only one thing to do.

CHAPTER 17

For the next two months, I worked hard to rebuild my reputation at school with the other kids. It was a serious attempt on my part to at least try to get back into the swing of things. For the first few weeks, I isolated myself, eating in the library, and pretended to work on my computer. However, as the days went on, I slowly connected with some of my friends. They realized they could talk to me and I wouldn't break down into hysterics. I'm not sure why, but I felt myself growing unemotional about the situation and more methodical about planning my revenge. The things that I used to worry about in school just didn't matter to me anymore.

I woke up this morning and got to school early so I could go to the library to pick out a book. I thought that if I could read, then it would take my mind off of everything else. At lunch, Monica and Lucy invited me to eat lunch in the courtyard under an oak tree. I unwrapped my turkey sandwich and began eating.

"Oh my gosh, did you hear about Janice?" Monica began.

"What do you mean?" I asked.

Monica and Lucy exchanged glances. "You mean you hadn't heard?"

"No, do you want me to guess?" I was getting frustrated.

"She escaped a near kidnapping two weeks ago." Lucy's eyes widened as she retold the story. "She was walking home, and a van pulled up beside her. A man got out and tried to pull her in."

"How do you know this?" I asked.

"Her mom and my mom go to the same church and her

mom broke down one day and told my mom." Lucy said.

"If it hadn't been for a neighbor of hers shouting and running toward them, she might have ended up like…" Lucy's voice trailed off.

I knew what she was going to say. "Like me, you mean."

"I'm so sorry, Marlene. I didn't mean-" Lucy slumped her shoulders.

"It's fine." I said. The truth was, I didn't care about this high school life anymore, or the gossip that fed into it.

Janice walked by and looked at me with a sad look on her face. She had such a strange expression that I grew suspicious of it. Was it sadness or guilt? I knew that if this story was true, then Janice had to be pretty shaken up about it. I could feel her pain and I was sorry that even a bully like her was subjected to such a traumatic experience.

"I actually feel bad for her," Monica said.

"Me too." Lucy agreed. "I've never liked her, but even

Janice didn't deserve something like that to happen to her.

This subject was bringing up anxiety for me, and I wanted to talk about anything other than this. I kept my cool, however, even though my mind was racing the entire time.

"Hey, I have an idea," Monica excitedly bounced on her knees. "How about we head down to D.C. tonight?"

"I don't think so," I said.

"Oh come on, it'll take your mind off of everything." Monica responded.

"Yeah, it'll be great! Oh, come on, come with us Marlene." Lucy chimed in.

The last thing I wanted to do was walk around downtown at night, but maybe they had a point. Maybe I needed to try to resume my normal life. "Okay, but promise me we stay together the entire time."

"Cross my heart," Lucy made a cross motion with her finger to her chest.

"Alright then." I conceded.

"Great!" Monica cheered. I'll pick up Lucy and then we will come by around eight."

I was afraid to get excited about this but I was looking forward to resuming some normalcy again. Maybe a night out with my two best friends would be good for me.

CHAPTER 18

Music blasted in the background as I got ready to go out. I tried my hardest to get into the mood, so it pleasantly surprised me when I realized I was dancing with the beat. The hot rollers burned my fingers as I rolled my hair around them. I stuck my index finger in my mouth to relieve the sting.

My hair didn't hold a curl worth a darn, but I missed getting ready to go out. The ritual helped build the excitement of the night. So tonight, I decided to try to put some effort into it and curl my hair.

I saw some smoke and was hoping I wasn't burning my hair off.

My mom peeked her head in my room. "Do you need anything?"

"No thanks." I said.

"I'm so happy to see you're going out. Monica and Lucy picking you up?" She asked.

"Yeah." She seemed excited for me and I appreciated that.

"Don't stay out too late." She reminded.

"I won't."

"And don't forget to text me to check in or I'll have to call you." She smiled.

"I got it, mom. I will." I said.

"You know, I bet your brother wouldn't mind tagging along. Do you want me to ask him?" I knew where she was going with this.

"No, mom. I will be fine. Monica, Lucy and I will stay

together the whole time."

"I love you and I'm proud of you." She gave me a kiss on the top of my head and left.

I finished my hair, gave it a quick spray, checked my lipstick and deemed myself officially 'dressed up' and ready. Monica texted me to say that she was waiting for me in my driveway.

I ran down the stairs and yelled over my shoulder as I opened the front door. "Bye!"

"Be careful!" They yelled back.

I ran out to the car where Monica and Lucy were waiting and jumped in the passenger side front seat. "Hey ladies. Ready?"

Monica has her mother's black SUV giving us each plenty of room to stretch out. Lucy's in the backseat, bouncing her head to the pop song playing. The whole way there we're singing and laughing. It was so nice not to worry about anything and just let go. Tonight, I didn't want to think too hard about anything. I just wanted to have a good time.

"Hey, I bet the college guys from Georgetown will be out tonight." Monica smiled and looked back at Lucy.

"Oh my gosh, I hope so." Lucy shook her fists in the air. "I could use a nice, hot distraction from Paul."

"What's wrong with you and Paul?" I asked without thinking. Lucy had dated Paul for close to three years. They were a couple I saw making it out of high school and into the world. It was a bit of a shock to hear that they were having problems.

"Tiffany Spencer, that's what's wrong with Paul." Lucy's expression changed from excited to jealous.

"Oh come off it, Lucy. It's not like he cheated on you. She's just the daughter of your mom's best friend."

"I don't get it," I said.

"She's mad at him because she just found out that Tiffany

accompanied them all on a camping trip over the summer and didn't mention it." Monica said.

"With those double D's, you'd think he'd remember to tell me." Lucy folded her hands across her torso.

"Well, I'm sure it wasn't anything serious." I offered. I had no idea what was going on and I honestly wasn't that interested in finding out.

We drove across the Potomac River and onto D.C. I recognized the monuments in the distance and knew we were getting close to D'Angelos. It was my favorite Italian restaurant. We had decided to go there for dinner. They had the best pizza I'd ever tasted. My parents had taken me there a few times. It was a D.C. staple.

I rolled down the window and took a deep breath allowing the night air to cool my face. I wanted to linger in this moment. It almost felt normal. Out with the girls, enjoying a simple night of teenage fun. I listened to the laughter that my friends traded back and forth and wish I could have that innocence back. I wanted to feel normal again. But in the back of my mind, it was always there. The events over the past several months. Even driving into D.C. had me scheming of ways to investigate the slavery ring.

We pulled up to D'Angelo's, got a table and ordered a pizza. "I'm so glad you guys dragged me out tonight. I wasn't sure if I wanted to come, but I'm glad I did." I flashed each of them a sincere smile.

"We're glad you came out." Lucy patted my arm.

"Yeah, it's not the same when you're not around. No fun at all. Glad you're getting back to your old self." Monica said.

I smiled in appreciation even though deep down I knew-- I would never be my old self again.

CHAPTER 19

D'Angelo's pizza was as delicious as I remember it. They added freshly sliced baby tomatoes and every bite I sank my teeth into was so good. It reminded me of when I was a kid and trips into D.C. were such a joy. It looked as though they'd added more ambience to the place having updated the decor. It now had more of an elegant atmosphere.

"Am I crazy or is our waiter a total babe?" Monica's eyebrows raised and lowered repeatedly.

Lucy and I giggled.

"I'm talking huba huba baby cakes." Monica said.

"He's probably a Georgetown college boy." I offered.

"I'd let him study me." Lucy said.

"Who's up for ice cream?" Monica asked.

"Aren't you full? I couldn't eat another bite." I said.

"I know a place on the way to the Washington monument. We can get ice cream cones. Come on you guys, it will be fun." Monica said.

"Oh why not," Lucy said. "I could use a good sugar rush."

We each laid cash on the table to cover the cost of the meal. Monica laid down a fifty dollar bill for the tip. Lucy and I gave her a look. "What?" She looked truly bewildered. "I believe in tipping well. Let's go."

Lucy and I snickered and walked out followed by Monica who was behind us. I followed them to the ice cream shop and then we headed down to the monument. It was a pleasant stroll. Lucy and Monica ate their cones as we passed by various sites. I took in the night air, breathing it in and appreciating this cool night air. I noticed that it was a little busier than usual downtown and wondered why. There were a lot of college students around, no doubt on their way to the local bars.

I was excited about seeing the monument again. It had been years since I'd last seen it. I think I was in eighth grade when I took a class field trip there. When we got to the monument, I noticed how beautiful it was lit up against the night sky.

Lucy placed her hand on the tall structure. "Do you think Washington was handsome?"

Monica and I looked at each other and laughed out loud. "What are you talking about?"

"I was just wondering if you thought he was handsome." Lucy said again.

Monica stared at Lucy. "Do you have daddy issues or something?"

"No, of course not. It was just a question, geez." Lucy walked ahead of us. "What's the big deal."

"I don't know, ask father time's girlfriend over here." Monica teased.

I laughed as we walked along the path. It was really nice to have these girls as my friends. I had a sudden surge of gratitude for them. I noticed they weren't asking me about what happened when I was kidnapped, and I appreciated that. They knew I needed space and they were giving it to me while taking me out and getting my mind off of it.

It was a beautiful evening. The trees were blowing in the chilly wind. I shivered and crossed my arms in front of me.

"Did you hear about Susie and Alex?" Monica asked me and before I had a chance to answer she continued. "They broke up. There was huge drama at school."

"No, I hadn't heard. What happened?" I asked.

"Susi found Alex and Andrew Fulton doing it. Walked right in on them." Lucy chimed in.

"Dude, I would have killed them both." Monica said.

"Wow, that's crazy," I offered.

"Pants down around his ankles and everything," Lucy added.

"That's terrible. How's Susi?" I asked.

"She hooked up with Tyler Benson at the fall festival to get back at Alex, and then Tyler and Alex got into this big fight at school. They suspended both of them for two weeks." Monica told the story as if she were front row in a movie theater watching it unfold.

"And now there's a rumor going around that Susi might be pregnant and she doesn't know who the father is." Lucy added.

"Good grief, that is a lot of drama." I said.

Our walk led us closer to the White House gates and as we approached, we saw a group of people standing around holding signs walking in a big circle. The sea of people and the collective noise from them was loud with agitation and anger. My curiosity grew. I wanted to see what they were marching about, so I headed toward the center of the group. It was obvious from their anti-war signs they were parading around chanting against the war in Syria. Monica, Lucy and I watched for a couple minutes until we saw the gates open and a black town car exit. The crowd turned aggressive, banging on the car and preventing it from. The situation was scary, and I made sure the three of us were far enough away from the crowd to avoid getting caught up in it. For a moment, my heart went out to the person or people in the car. I wondered if they were scared, too.

As the car turned the corner in front of us, camera flashes illuminated the figure inside. My stomach dropped and adrenaline shot through my veins. I recognized the person in the car behind the tinted windows. It was Homeland Secretary Hullman. My jaw dropped and I froze.

"What's wrong, Marlene?" Monica watched my face.

My fists clenched as tears filled my eyes. Anger filled my heart but I couldn't move.

"Tell me what it is." Monica stepped in front of me.

Lucy noticed us and stepped into our circle. "Are you okay? What's wrong, Marlene?"

I couldn't tell them. I couldn't admit the man I was looking for was in that car. The man who tried to sell me into slavery. The car drove past us and disappeared into the streets of D.C. I collapsed to the ground, unable to stop the stream of tears exiting my eyes.

Monica and Lucy bunt down and grabbed my arms, trying to help me to my feet.

My body was limp. I didn't have the will to help myself up. I felt utterly defeated. One protester noticed me, reached out and touched my shoulder. "I know. The war in Syria is awful. Don't worry yourself sick about it, though."

I tried to smile at her kindness, but I could only cry. This was unbelievable, and the reality of him being in such close personal proximity to me took all my energy and breath. I could do nothing but sit in the street weeping.

I had to get a grip. My nose was running, and I wiped it with my sleeve before shifting my head back to stop crying.

"Please tell us what's wrong, Marlene." Monica begged.

"I'm so sorry. We were having so much fun. I'm sorry I ruined our evening." I offered.

"You didn't ruin anything," Lucy bent down and wrapped her arm around my shoulder.

Marlene picked herself up "I'm okay guys," she said.

"What is it?" What's wrong Monica asked.

"I'm just upset…. About Syria…" it was the only thing I can think of fast enough. I couldn't tell them the truth. I couldn't tell anyone the truth.

"Let's go home," Lucy said.

"No no.. I'll just call my mom. You guys can go out with me."

"There's no way we're leaving you by yourself out here." Monica insisted.

"Yeah, not a chance." Lucy said.

"I promise I will be fine. I don't want you both missing out because of me." I responded.

"It's absolutely out of the question, Marlene. We're serious. We are not leaving you here." Monica put her hands on her hips.

"Okay, fine. You don't have to leave me here, but can you give me some time to myself?" I asked. "Go on to the club and I will catch up. I just want to sit here for awhile."

They both gave me sideways glances.

"Guys, I promise I will be fine. I just need some time alone.

Monica and Lucy looked at each other before Monica spoke up. "Okay fine. We will give you some time to yourself, but we are just up the street at Hitch's Sports Bar, okay? If you need us we will be there."

"Thank you." I said. "I appreciate it. They both gave me a hug before turning and starting off down the road toward the sports bar.

I watched them walk down the sidewalk until they disappeared. I shot up and looked down the street toward the town car. My palms were sweaty, and I felt my knees weaken at the rage that was fast consuming me. I swallowed hard and took off down the street in the direction the car was traveling. I pumped my arms and moved my feet as fast as I could, but the distance between us was too far. Hullman's car turned the corner, and I followed it. When I got around the corner, I saw the black town car being blocked by protesters. They were screaming anti-war chats and surrounding the car. His driver tried to drive but stopped as protesters jumped on the hood of his car. They had the entire road completely blocked off and refused to allow Hullman's car to pass.

My body was shaking. I ran closer to the car and saw a rock on the ground. I picked it up and threw it as hard as I could into the rear window of the car. It shattered the black window and I saw Hullman's face in shock as he turned to see me staring back at him. I shook with rage as spit flew out of my mouth. Fury was the only thing I felt, and I didn't hold myself back. I jumped on the back of his car and banged on the trunk as I tried to climb into the rear window. I wanted to kill him right there.

The crowd screamed as I kicked out the remaining glass and tried to crawl in to get at him. I felt several hands grab various parts of my body and try to pull me away from him. When I looked back, I saw they were protesters. "I know what you did, Hullman!" I screamed his name loud with every grief-stricken word I had inside me.

"Damn girl" yelled a protestor.

The crowd died down to watch what I was going to do next. I tried to catch my breath as I stared Hullman down. He stared right back at me but showed no recognition.

"Yeah let's mess his car up!" Another protester screamed.

Everyone who was standing around, picked up rocks and began throwing them at his car. I stuck my middle finger out at him and smiled. I wanted him to remember me.

That's when I heard the police sirens growing louder. The cars attached to them came speeding around the corner. I followed the protesters and ran down the street. The crowd ran in different directions. I tried to keep pace with the rest of the mob but I stopped instead and looked around. I saw Hullman's car dented with serious scratches and broken glass. . That reality made me want to smile. Marlene runs with the protesters. But stopped and turned around. Hullman's gaze followed me as I ran down the street. I looked into his eyes with pure hatred. Hullman sat there emotionless, unable to believe what he was seeing was real life.

I turned back around and focused on where I was running to. I headed up the streets of D.C and saw a couple of protesters caught and getting arrested. I knew I had put myself in real trouble, and the last thing I needed was to get arrested. I ran four more blocks and heard at least four more cop cars coming after me from behind. Thinking quick, I made a sharp left turn and ran into a coffee shop. I tried to look like I fit in waiting for my turn at a coffee. It appeared to work as police cars passed the shop. They blew past as cars tried their best to get out of their way.

I ordered an ice coffee and then sat down. Unfortunately, I could do little to save the protesters who were being arrested right outside the shop. I watched as they were being zip tied and put into police cars. There was nowhere left to go. I stayed calm and pretended to be playing a game on my phone. I regulated my breathing and reminded myself that if I didn't panic, then there was no reason the cops would find me. I would wait until everything died down and then meet up with Lucy and Monica at the sports bar.

Nights like this used to never happen to me. Now it seems I'm all about the drama.

CHAPTER 20

The server sat the white mug down on the table in front of me. The steam rising off the top warned me to treat it carefully. Last time I ordered a tea, I underestimated how hot it would be and burned my tongue. I couldn't taste anything for almost a week. Touching the outer white ceramic shell, I tested the heat with my fingers, careful not to linger. The temperature seemed cool enough, so I took a sip from my mug.

People were scattered throughout the diner, not too close to each other but close enough to overhear their conversations if one should choose to do so. People watching had always been a favorite of mine. When my parents would take me on vacation, I would sit in a chair at the airport waiting for our flight and watch hundreds of people pass in front of me. I found it intriguing watching people walk from one place to another going on about their life, oblivious that a stranger was watching them.

I sat in the coffee shop watching the blue and red swirling lights fade into the horizon as the police pulled out and drove away from the scene. It took me a minute to realize I had run away with my thoughts. It was easy for me to do. With everything that was going on, I needed the distraction. I needed time to think about what I was going to do. The clock on the wall pointed well past midnight. I should have been on my way home. But I wasn't sure that I wanted to go home. The alternative would be to go somewhere else, but where? I didn't feel like I would be safe anywhere else.

The server dropped a cup and saucer on the tile floor, causing it to shatter into pieces and me to jump. My initial reaction was fear, followed by anger for being scared. I didn't like loud noises, especially the ones that came out from nowhere.

Across from me, a man was shaking a sugar packet. He tore the top off before sprinkling it over his coffee. I felt like I was in a movie. These things didn't happen to everyday people. There was nothing normal about any of this.

I replayed the events from earlier in my head. Hullman's car driving away from me like the coward he was. I wasn't sorry about what I did. In fact, I was glad about it. Every time I thought about hearing his voice from the back of the van, I got angry all over again. This time it was a calm rage welling up inside of me. I'd gotten that close to Hullman once. I could do it again. There was nothing that was going to stop me from getting my revenge.

I pulled out my phone and logged into my social media. My heart dropped as I saw what was trending in the top spot on the local news app. "Secretary of Homeland

Security attacked by violent protester." There was a big picture of me. My eyes scanned the room as my heart began to beat fast and my palms started to sweat. It terrified me that someone would recognize me. I ran into the bathroom. The room had wall to wall tiles in a brown and peach color and was terribly gaudy. I wasn't paying too much attention, trying to get into the stall and hide myself. My hands were shaking. I was in full blown panic mode.

How long would it be before the police would come looking for me? What would happen once they found me?I tried to calm my breathing and think through the situation, but the only thing I could think of was calling my mother. Maybe she would understand if I explained to her what happened. I pulled out my phone and dialed her number. It rang several times before I heard a soft voice on the other end.

"Hello?"

"Mom! I need you to pick me up."

"Marlene? What's wrong?"

"Please. There's no time. Just meet me at the coffee shop on Washington Avenue." I hung up.

My nerves were frazzled.I stood outside of the coffee shop until my mom pulled up. Once she pulled up to the corner, I looked both ways before walking out from the shadows, I pulled my gray hoodie over my head. Out of the corner of my eye, I saw a lady walk out of the coffee shop and look at me. She stared as our eyes met, and it felt like she might have recognized me. I felt my anxiety swell in my throat as I ran to my mom's black sedan, opened the door and got inside.

"Let's go!" I screamed.

I tried to take a deep breath, but the weight of my worries made it difficult for me to inhale. I could feel my legs weaken and I was glad that I was sitting down.

"What's going on?" She asked.

Before I could explain, my phone lit up, followed by my ringtone blaring. I didn't look for it or pull it out of my pocket. I knew it couldn't be good news, whoever it was from. Fear gripped me and I clasped my hands to my chest. My mind was racing. I couldn't think fast enough about what to do. My phone stopped ringing and about a second later, my mom's phone lit up. I looked at my mom and she looked back at me before reaching into her pocket and pulling it out. She pushed the green button and put the phone up to her ear.

I waited to hear her speak so that I could figure out who she was talking to, but her expression made it clear enough. Her face dropped as her eyes widened. Her mouth opened and I grew impatient. "What is it, mom?"

"The police are at our house looking for you," she said. "You attacked the secretary of homeland security car?"

I watched as we passed the lights on the interstate. The tail lights of the car in front of us glowed red against the faint evening sky. I looked out of the window up at the faint stars and wished I was anyone else other than who I was right now. Tears welled up as a feeling of powerlessness overcame me.

I slumped down in my seat as I cried. I could feel my mother's eyes judging me and my self-pity turned to anger. "Yes, mom! I did! And I'm proud of it!"

Her eyes narrowed as she tried to enforce her authority over me. I saw the disappointment in her face and it conflicted me between the guilt I felt over letting my parents down and the anger that this had happened to me. It was still happening.

"Are you stupid! He's a government official! Are you really that upset over the war in Syria? You never talked about politics at home." She yelled as her hands waved wildly.

She looked at me and then back at the road ahead as she drove, expecting me to answer. I realized she thought I was reacting to the protest and politics of this evening. I calmly

147

lowered my voice in an attempt to reason with her and correct her understanding of why I did what I did. "Mom, please listen to me. I'm not crazy. While I was gone three months ago, Hullman was the man who tried to buy me."

"For the international pedophile ring?" She asked. "You went on and on and on about this already. Did you take your meds today?"

My heart broke that she could treat me this cruelly. I resented her lack of empathy for what I've been through.

"No mom, the feds threatened my life in front of the school to not tell. Why don't you believe me?"

"Enough!" She shouted.

"But mom…"

"Not another word!" She continued driving, her face beet red.

I wiped the tears from my face, embarrassed that I had dared to let her see that I was vulnerable. It was clear that

I wouldn't be able to trust my mother anymore. I sniffled as a new wave of crying overtook me despite my best efforts. The feeling of betrayal slowly burning inside. How could she not believe me?

If the police were already at my house, then I knew they would take me into custody. That means I was going to jail. I silently thought about what jail would be like and if I would be at risk of getting hurt in there. Would another prisoner try to attack me. I continued sobbing. My life was over. I thought about all the things I would miss out on by being in jail. My wedding. Having children. Going to college like every other typical kid. There was nothing I could do to change my fate now.

My mom turned the steering wheel toward the driveway as the front tires followed in the same direction. She pulled up to the garage door and turned the ignition off. My heart dropped as I saw the police cars with their lights flashing and the officers standing in the yard tense up as we pulled in. I clenched my fists together until my knuckles were

149

white and took a deep breath. The two uniformed officers in the front lawn were drastically different from each other. One was taller with large biceps. He obviously worked out. The cop next to him was quite a bit shorter and wore a military haircut.

They both looked intimidating to me. I looked at my mom as we sat there hoping for guidance on what to do. "Well..." She nodded her head in the direction of the police officers.

I got out of the car as the taller officer walked up to me. "Put your hands on your head!"

I was shocked at the intensity of his words and did what he told me to do. He grabbed my arm and put handcuffs on me.

"Mom!" I screamed.

"Don't resist, Marlene. Just do what they say." She answered, her hands over her mouth.

They put me in the back of the police car and shut the door.

150

The emptiness filled me and threatened to choke me. Everyone thought I was a troublemaker. They probably thought I was making all of this up, too. After a few minutes, the officers got into the car and drove off to jail. There was a wire divider between the front and back seats. It felt like I was sitting in a cage. I'd never felt more alone.

When I got there, they took all my information. Then they led me to a room with black lines on the wall. They made me stand in front of it and took my picture. The bright flash burned my eyes, and I stood there humiliated in front of all these strangers who probably just assumed I was a guilty criminal. No doubt this story was already running on the evening news. I'm sure the media will say that I assaulted Hullman.

After what seemed like hours, they gave me a prison uniform and made me put it on. It was neon orange and every bit as embarrassing as it sounds. I followed an officer down a dark corridor past other cells and other female prisoners yelling at me. They were trying to rattle me, which was working. But on the outside, I held my head high and ignored them as I walked by. In my hands were my bed linens. I held my tears back until I got into my cell and the officer left. What was I going to do now? I broke down, feeling like I was the only person I could depend on.

"Better not let nobody see you crying like a baby in here." A voice echoed from the across the cell. A shadow stepped out and a girl with blonde dreadlocks and a dragon tattoo on her neck stood there looking down at me. Her tattoo looked older, which was strange because she looked so young. Something told me she'd been here a few times before.

I stayed on my side of the cell and tried to ignore her.

"You hear me? Dry those tears, crybaby." She slowly walked over to where I was sitting on one of the cots.

I sniffled. "Just leave me alone, okay?"

"I don't know what you have to cry about, anyway." She taunted. "It's not like you'll be in here long."

Her comment struck me. Had she recognized me on the news? I wiped my eyes and lifted my head. "What do you mean?"

"A rich girl like you? Your parents will be here to bail you out in no time." She brushed a dreadlock off her shoulder.

"I'm not rich," I protested.

"Yeah, right? That cashmere sweater you're wearing with the diamond stud earrings gives you away." The girl grinned.

I looked down at what I was wearing. It was the first time I'd realized what I wore gave off an impression on other people. I brushed that thought aside as she stared at me, her yellow teeth daring me to snicker. "What are you in for?"

It was only after I asked that I realized I probably shouldn't have. I didn't know proper prison etiquette. Her smile dropped and a blank look came over her. I tried to think of something else to say. "What's your name?

"What do you care?" She said.

"I was just trying to make polite conversation." I answered.

"What's your name?" She countered.

"Marlene. And you?" I watched her face as she debated whether or not she wanted to be nice to me.

"Adel." She answered.

"Like the singer?"

"No. Not like the singer." She rolled her eyes and jumped on the top bunk.

"So what are you in for?" I asked again, feeling a little braver this time.

"I hot-wired a car and led the cops on a chase around town." Her eyes lit up as if she was proud of what she had done.

I don't know why, but I found that exciting. I would never in a million years steal a car and run from the police, but the daydream was enough to keep me entertained in here.

"Why did you do that?"

"Because I could." She laughed. "What are you in here for?"

"You wouldn't believe me if I told you." I said.

"Try me." Adel said.

"I assaulted Secretary Hullman." I said.

"Who?" She asked.

"You know, Secretary Hullman?" I waited for a spark of recognition to ignite in her brain but it seemed she really didn't know who I was talking about. I explained what happened.

"Huh," she said. "Gotta say, I never would have thought someone like you had it in you."

I took that as a compliment. I woke up sometime later to the sound of whispers. My eyes opened, but I kept my body still. I was facing the wall so no one could tell. It sounded like a couple of people were standing in front of

155

my cell speaking to each other in low voices. When the voices stopped, I waited a second to make sure they were gone before turning over to catch a glimpse of the voices. There were two men in black suits walking around the jail. My heart stopped. They must be agents of some kind. Secret Service perhaps? Whoever they were, they stuck out like a sore thumb. My chest tightened and my breathing became labored. Something told me they were there for me. They had to be. I closed my eyes, trying to remember a time before all of this happened. I wished more than anything that I could go back there and redo things. I never would have given Dmitri the time of day either. I hope he was somewhere right now being tortured. I fell asleep again and somehow managed to sleep through the night. Somehow imagining Dmitri in extreme pain helped.

CHAPTER 21

"Hey! Get dressed. Your parents are here. You're going home." The officer placed my clothes on the bench in my cell before locking the door and walking off.

I jumped up, excited at the news. I hopped over to get my clothes and put them on quickly before any of the officers returned. When I was escorted to the front of the police station, my mother and father were there waiting. They each took turns hugging me.

"We're so glad you're okay." My father placed his hands

on both sides of my face and gently squeezed before giving me another hug. "You are okay, aren't you? They didn't mistreat you, did they?"

I shook my head no.

They carried on looking me over to be sure I was telling the truth as I noticed two men in black suits in the distance. This wasn't a coincidence. They were definitely following me.

"Here are your discharge papers," the male officer handed them to me but my mom grabbed them before he could.

"I'll take those." She smiled.

"You have a court date in two months." The officer reminded me.

My mom gathered me and my belongings, and with my dad we all left the police station. When we got home, I went to my room and laid on my bed. I could hear them arguing about how much the bail was and how they were going to have to spend more money on a lawyer. I couldn't stand it anymore. I couldn't understand how they had so little empathy for what I'd been through? I jumped off my bed, swung open my door and stood in the hallway staring at them both. "What about me? Why don't you believe me he's the man who tried to purchase me!"

"It's not that we don't believe you, sweetie." My dad began but was interrupted by my mom.

"Can you prove that? You need to find proof fast young lady, your court date is in 60 days." My mom responded as she walked downstairs.

My mind started racing about finding evidence. I looked at my phone to see that my face was all over social media. There had to be at least fifty missed calls from my friends and numbers I didn't recognize. Possibly the media is trying to get a quote. I scrolled through my posts and it was the same. A dozen or more messages and posts with my mugshot. I threw the phone across the room and drew my knees into my chest. Nobody at school will ever let me forget this. I felt myself rocking and whimpering as streams of tears rolled down my cheeks.

My mom came into my room. "The school called, you just got suspended until further notice." She stared at me as I tried to ignore her. "Anything to say?" She asked.

I remained silent until she left, shutting the door behind her. I didn't want to talk to her right now. Not after what she'd said to me. I heard my dad from downstairs yell "Marlene is on TV."

I closed my eyes and laid down on my bed, fully aware that my life was over. I would never get hired anywhere, never get married or go to college. I will be friendless for the rest of my life. Maybe it would be better if I wasn't here anymore. I shook my head at such dark thoughts, realizing that I couldn't give up that easily. It was late, and I needed to sleep. But first, I had to figure out where I would find evidence to prove my case. I wore myself out thinking about it and managed to wake up at six the next morning to the sound of my parents heading off for work.

I woke up the next morning and walked downstairs. I sat on the couch and turned on the television. I flipped through the channels until I found a news station that was talking about the incident. My face along with other protestors were plastered everywhere. There was a sound bite of Hullman being interviewed.

"I was afraid for my life. We need to put them in jail for a very long time" he said, standing in front of his damaged car. My anxiety morphed into anger. I was going to get him. I had nothing to lose anymore. I heard a car passing by outside. I made my way to the window. It was the same car that threatened me two months ago. I noticed his face through the window as he was staring into my house. I quickly closed the window blinds. I stood there for five minutes grasping the situation. I went back upstairs to my room. How was I going to get the evidence I needed?

I went onto my computer and spent most of the day

looking closely at what people were saying online. I noticed that my social media followers jumped to one hundred fifty thousand. My eyes widened in disbelief. Then I realized how much power I actually had. Quickly, I hit the record button.

"Hey guys, its Marlene, I'm the girl you've seen on TV. An international pedophile ring sponsored by the US government has kidnapped me. I was bought for tens of thousands of dollars by George Hullman. I escaped and confronted my kidnapper two days ago. I need your help guys. They are in front of my house." I pointed my phone outside where the FBI car was sitting. "I need evidence guys so we can show the world the truth!"

I uploaded it on my social media account and watched as my followers went crazy. I made two more videos on social media explaining the entire story of how I got kidnapped. Those videos gained one hundred thousand views within two hours. My comment sections began exploding with images of Dmitri and his family in Russia. I was stunned.

There were people who claimed to know more information about them. I got excited and finally felt like I might be making progress.

What would this mean? What if the authorities could actually track them down and bring them to justice? I breathed in a sigh of hopeful excitement, afraid to get too excited about it but also needing something to look forward to. I'd been living in a consistent state of stress for a while now. I needed some sort of light at the end of the tunnel. Laying on my bed, I watched as the comments and views on my social media soared.

CHAPTER 22

It was five in the afternoon when my parents came home. I heard my dad walking up the steps and then knock on my door. "What are all these posts online? What is that about?"

"Have you seen the comments, dad? Do you know what they are saying? I jumped up and showed him several posts on my feed. "They're giving me useful clues about the kidnapping."

A look of understanding spread across my father's face. He was finally understanding what was going on.

My eyes open wide as a message made a ding in my inbox. I opened it. It was from the family of a bystander who died during the crossfire when I was rescued. His name was Adam Sylvester. As I read it, it explained that he went missing by the very place that I was talking about on social media. I showed my father.

"I told you I'm not lying!!"

My father called my mother upstairs. Together, we read the message. It explained that the police were acting strange and they found out that all the video cameras in the area were gone. "Something's going on here," I said.

I sent them a message back about what happened to me. This person responded with a link to a video that showed the son recording a video about finding justice for his dad. His video had 500,000 views.

My story was now at two million views. My comment section was filled with "Q Anon" conspiracy theories and Pizza Gate. A cult-like following was forming around me as I continued making video after video. My viewers began finding clues on the internet. It was incredible. For the first time, I felt validated about what happened to me.

"I'm calling a lawyer," my mom said. She called her co-worker's husband and asked if he would come over. As she was on the phone, I went over to the window and looked outside. The FBI car was no longer outside. That made me suspicious. I realized that my social media posts hadn't been deleted, which was also weird. It was viral now. Maybe there wasn't anything they could do to stop it. *Good*, I thought.

I told the lawyer everything that had happened from the beginning. We sat in the living room and talked for a couple hours. I showed him the social media posts and all the comments leading to several clues. He asked if I would save these messages and I agreed. I began taking screenshots from my phone.

"In the morning I will reach out to Adam Sylvester's

family." He said.

It felt like it was finally all coming together and on the right track. After the lawyer left, my parents and I stood there stunned. We were in disbelief at what was happening. I might actually get justice for what happened to me. And with any luck, maybe it will change things for others who won't have to go through what I did.

I was so happy that my parents finally seemed to fully believe me. I also received texts from my friends and my older brother in college who were also believing me, too. I held the phone close to my heart, closed my eyes and gave a moment of thanks.

A loud noise burst through my bedroom window, shattering the glass. The bullet missed me and exploded into the wall behind me. I dropped to the ground and crawled to the window to see a black car driving away. My parents ran into the room. "Are you okay?" My mother screamed.

"They're after me!" I yelled.

My father pulled out his phone and dialed the police. I picked up my phone and hit record. I showed my new audience the bullet hole. Within minutes, the comment section went wild.

CHAPTER 23

"Can I come in?" The lawyer stood on our front steps.

"Yes, of course." My father said.

"I brought a tape of the FBI pointing a gun at Marlene. I went to the school and got it." The lawyer said.

My father played the tape as I recorded it on my phone for social media.

"See, right there?" The lawyer said. "The license plate on Hullman's car matches the car that was in the driveway. The lawyer matched the license plate with the homeland security car on his driveway of his house.

He sat at our dining table with us throughout the day, helping us put the case together. I grabbed the remote and turned on the national news. They were talking about alt right conspiracy theories rocking social media.

I went onto my phone and found what seemed to be more hate comments calling me a racist. This was right after the news story talked about me. Hundreds of posts filled my timeline calling me a white supremacist. They insinuated that I was lying to gain attention and notoriety. My follower count plummeted. I tapped into my inbox and saw that it was filled with hate messages.

"They are censoring me!" I yelled. "I'm not a white supremacist!!" This was all too much. I broke down in the middle of the living room.

Mom came over and wrapped her arms around me. "I believe you," she said as she wiped away my tears. "It's alright, Marlene. We will win this thing."

CHAPTER 24

"The Sylvester family is twenty minutes away. They stopped at the Seafood Shack to grab a bite to eat and then they will head here." Our lawyer announced.

I said a silent prayer that they would make it here safely. Things were getting crazy. The truth was unraveling quickly. We needed the Sylvester's story to strengthen the evidence we were gathering against Hullman. I felt a pang of excitement that we were so close.

A couple of hours passed and the Sylvester family still wasn't here. I started getting nervous. Were we just too uptight waiting for them, or was something really wrong? Our lawyer kept trying to call the family, but they didn't answer. That didn't sound right to me. If they were eating, they'd still have their phones and could answer a call. Especially because they knew we were waiting for them.

"Let's go to the restaurant and meet them there," my mother said.

"What if they changed their mind?" I asked.

"Let's find out." My mother took my hand and walked me out the door.

"We will stay here with the lawyer." My father yelled after.

We drove toward the restaurants and as we got closer; we noticed several ambulances and sirens in front of the restaurant. I cupped my hands to my mouth, terrified that what I was thinking was actually happening. My stomach dropped as we approached. I knew it was them. I knew the Sylvester family was dead.

My mom parked the car. I jumped out and ran toward the

restaurant. My mom caught up and grabbed me. "No!"

I saw on the ground several dead bodies. There was blood pooled around them with bullet wounds on one of their foreheads. My body slumped to the ground, the tears unable to stop. Andrew Sylvesters family. His 15-year-old son and his mother, whom I had been contacting online. My mother and I began crying as we held each other.

"It was a robbery gone wrong" one paramedic said.

"No, they were murdered!" I yelled.

My mother continued sobbing. I choked back tears and took out my phone, taking a picture to post on my profile. It was morbid, but I had to stay strong enough to get the truth out there. I helped my mother to her feet. We got back into our car. My mom took out her phone. "What are you doing, mom?"

"I'm calling your father." She answered.

A few seconds passed. "He's not answering. He always answers his phone. Especially right now." She said.

My stomach felt queasy as I thought about the worst that could have happened to him. I checked my post and realized that it wasn't getting any likes, shares or comments. "Look mom, I'm shadow banned. Nobody's seeing my posts now."

"We need to get home." My mother turned the key in the ignition, put the car in gear and squealed tires taking off and heading home.

As we approached the house, I noticed something was not right. "Why is the front door open?" I asked.

We jumped out of the car and raced inside. My mother reached the front door first. "Hunny!? Hunny!? We're home. Answer me!!"

I started crying again and put my face in my knees rocking back and forth on the floor. I knew deep down what had happened.

"No! Please God, no!" My mom shrieked a powerful and painful scream. It startled me off the floor and I ran to where she was in the house. There at the kitchen table sat my father and our lawyer- dead. Each had bullet holes in their heads.

"No! Daddy no!" I screamed.

Mom touched Dad's face and cried. "We've got to go to the police." She was focused despite her eyes red and swelling.

"Nobody is going to help us! The police will not help, they are with them!" I yelled.

"We're next, mom! We've gotta get out of this town!" . I tried to pull her away from my father's body.

"I don't wanna leave him!" She yelled.

"He's gone, momma. We've got to go or we will be next." I pleaded. I turned around as I heard a car come up the street, it's engine revving up. It bounced as it hit our driveway. "Someone is coming!" I yelled.

My mom was now in pain. She ignored me and continued sobbing over her dead husband. It was all I could do not to do the same, but I knew we were in danger. I heard the front door open and jerked my head in the noise's direction. It was too late. We were going to die next. I clenched my eyes closed, waiting for the bullet to hit me next.

CHAPTER 25

"Marlene?" A familiar voice echoed in the foyer.

"Janice?" It made little sense. I opened my eyes and ran into the hall to see her standing there. It surprised me to see my enemy at my house.

"I don't have time to explain. Both of you- get in my car. Hurry! They're coming!" Janice yelled.

I didn't think except to collect the paperwork from the dinner table. I noticed that the case paperwork was gone. Somebody must have taken it.

"Hey, let's go!" Janice yelled.

I grabbed my mom by the shoulders and hurried her out the door. She didn't want to let go of my dad. "Leave me here, Marlene! Let me die with your father!"

"I need you, mom. Don't give up on me. We have to go now!" I forcefully pulled her off my father and rushed her into the back seat of Janice's small red sedan.

Janice pulled her car out of the driveway and squealed, tires driving off as fast as she could down the neighborhood streets. I noticed the FBI cars going in the opposite direction towards our house. I ducked just to ensure they wouldn't see us.

"Why are you helping us!?" I asked.

Janice didn't answer. Instead, she kept her focus on the road, turning and sliding into back roads.

"Turn your phone off!" Janice instructed.

"Why? My mom asked.

"Because they will find you!" Janice answered.

My mom and I scrambled to get our phones out of our pockets and turn them off. My mom's hands were shaking. "It's alright mom. It will be alright."

My mom stared into space seemingly in shock. Janice drove us deep into the woods of Virginia. I tried to breathe deeply so that I could sort my thoughts. Why was Janice here? And why was she helping us? None of this made sense.

"Marlene, I believe you." Janice said. "I always have."

"What are you talking about?" I asked.

"My dad works at the White House with the President," Janice said. "I know everything. I knew about Dmitri's family. I know about the trafficking ring. I'm gonna help you."

Janice turned into what looked to be a homemade campsite. She shut the engine off but kept her hands on the wheel, then let out a deep sigh. "My family is involved in the trafficking ring, Marlene. I know everything. I'm so sorry for what happened to you." Janice sobbed.

"What are you saying, Janice?" I asked in horror.

"I can't do this anymore! My parents bring girls to my house and keep them in our basement. They threatened to send me to a boarding school if I said anything. I'm terrified of my parents and I see these girls every day! I can't do it!" Janice screamed as she hits the steering wheel.

"You're saying you had girls under your house too?" I asked in disbelief.

"Yes, Marlene! Many people in our school have victims under their house," said Janice. "This ring is bigger than you think. They sell thousands of girls a day here in DC."

I was shocked.

"You mean hundreds of people know about this happening!? Even at your school!?" My mom asked.

"There were kids at our school who knew I was under Dmitris house?" The realization hit hard at how deep the

180

betrayal went.

"Yes. Some kids at our school knew you were under his house. I did too. Marlene, I'm so sorry." Janice's sobs got louder. "My parents are part of the satanic cult."

"Why are thousands of girls being sold only in DC?" I asked, trying to swallow the bile I felt rising in my throat. "This makes little sense, Janice. There are not enough politicians for all the girls." I scratched my head.

Janice sighed. "They sacrifice hundreds of people a day under the White House as part of a ritual."

"Sacrifice?" I repeated her word.

"Yes, Marlene. I can't live with myself knowing you were going to be sold. That's why I paid the gang to let you free by the border." She said.

"Wait, you sent them?" It was all so overwhelming. I was trying to grasp everything she was saying.

"Yes. I knew where you were and where you were headed

to. I couldn't live with myself knowing you'd end up dead. Even though we were enemies." She said.

"Wow." That was all I could get out of my mouth. I sat back, astonished that Janice out of all people would save me.

"I know we've been enemies for years, but we need to work together on this one, Marlene. We're going to expose them together." Janice grabbed my hand and squeezed it.

My mom passed out in the back seat as Janice and I continued talking about what we were going to do next.

CHAPTER 26

I awoke to the sound of my mother crying. Janice slowly stirred awake. "Where are we?" My mother asked.

"Somewhere in the countryside," Janice answered. "We should keep moving. They will look for us." Janice put the car in gear and drove out of the woods. Down the road was a truck stop. She pulled in and parked. "We can get a shower, gas and some food here. My mother and I shook our heads in agreement.

My mother followed me into the station where we grabbed several different items including food. When the clerk gave us our total, my mom pulled out her card and was about to slide it in the car reader when I stopped her. "They can trace us. Use cash."

My mother nodded and pulled out cash to cover the cost.

As we headed back to the car, I saw Janice on the phone talking with someone. She hung up when we approached. "Who were you talking to?" I asked as I remembered Janice had told us to turn our phones off earlier.

"Where are you taking us?" My mother asked cautiously.

"We're going to meet the resistance," Janice answered.

"I just saw your phone." I said.

"No Marlene, this was a text from the resistance." She unlocked the screen and showed the text. She tapped his profile, and it was a tall, husky man with a beard holding a huge Q Anon flag.

I blinked. "Q Anon? That wacky conspiracy theory? Didn't they storm the capital a few years ago?"

"No, this is a real underground movement. We're gonna expose the pedophile ring in Washington DC," Janice explained. She turned the car on and backed out of the parking lot. My Mom stayed silent in the back seat as I rode in the front.

I wasn't sure about all of this. Something didn't feel right. I couldn't put my finger on it, but there was something about Janice's story that I found suspicious. I decided I would keep an eye on her. Unfortunately, I had little a choice but to go with her to see where it would lead. If she was telling the truth, then she had a lot of evidence she could produce. That made her my strongest witness and my new best friend.

CHAPTER 27

We drove for what seemed like hours into rural Virginia. The forest was thick and lush. I couldn't help but think that it was the perfect place to hide. Janice turned down a back road that wasn't paved. The three of us continued on for what seemed to be another twenty minutes until a small wooden cabin appeared at the end of the road. We pulled up to it and stopped. My anxiety swelled, waiting for what would happen next. Was this a trap?

A man walked out of the wooden house. It was the man in the photo on Janice's phone. I was relieved and got out of the car.

"I'm Robert," he said.

Robert looked like a stereotypical redneck with a Confederate flag on his hat. He was wearing a plaid shirt and dirty blue jeans.

"Mom, come on." I nudged my mom. She didn't move. She was awake, but she didn't move. "Cmon mom!" I raised my voice hoping to knock her out of her shock, but she still didn't move. "Mom, you need to be strong for me. We are going to get them back for what they did to dad." She slowly turned her head until her eyes met mine and then nodded her head.

The four of us walked in the front door. There were around fifteen people inside. Q Anon wallpapers filled the entire walls of the living room. I felt a little uncomfortable walking in. There were guns everywhere with a huge Trump 2020 flag in the middle of the living room above the fireplace. A confederate flag was on the ceiling. This scared me a little. I wasn't sure what we were stepping into.

"We are close to exposing this whole thing to Marlene," said Robert. "Thanks to Janice here, we know the date of the next ritual under the White House. We're planning to raid the capital again on that day to expose everything."

Janice smiles. "Thanks to you Marlene, many people online are on board for this movement" She smiled at my mom. "We will take them down once and for all!"

Robert looked at me. "We have over 25,000 people coming to the capital with guns. We're going to take those devil worshiping pedophile elites. It'll be a surprise attack."

"But I'm being canceled on social media. I'm being called a white supremacist every day. How do we know all these people are coming?" I asked.

"We use other websites with VPN's and we have special chat boards. We know they are coming. Thousands have booked their flights," Robert replied.

I smiled and then jumped with excitement. "I can't believe

this is happening. We're going to get justice!"

"And it's all because of you Marlene, without your videos online we wouldn't have had so many people join our cause." A woman sitting on the couch said. She was wearing a cowboy hat and country boots.

"So this 'Q Anon' isn't some random conspiracy theory online? It's real?" I asked.

"Yes, Marlene, it's real. The media, big tech companies, and the government are all in it. We have a few people on the inside who are in the resistance. Like your friend Janice over here." Robert pointed at a smiling Janice.

"Come with me." Robert asked. We followed him down the hall into the basement. There was a small bedroom with over 20 rifles on the walls. The woman from the living room brought them some clothes and a blanket. "Thanks," I said.

My mom finally smiled. "Everything's going to be alright, mom." I assured her.

There was a knock on the door. "Come in," I said.

"We got some food," Robert came with a plate of barbecue.

I grabbed the plate from him. "Thank you."

He handed a plate to my mother. "Sorry, I'm on the Keto diet, red meat isn't good for me." My mother responded.

"Yall city people are weird" Robert closed the door behind him.

I gave my mom a look. "What?" She asked.

"There probably isn't a lot of food. You'd better eat what they have." I said.

I walked over to the bed and unfolded the linens. I made the bed and laid down falling asleep without finishing my dinner.

CHAPTER 28

I opened my eyes, tried to swallow, and realized my throat was dry. I sat up in bed, trying to get my bearings to remember where I was. I yawned and stretched and grabbed the plate on the bedside table that I had used to finish the last piece of chicken from last night and brought it upstairs.

Trying not to make a lot of noise, I noticed everybody was asleep on the couches. I tiptoed to the kitchen and put my plate in the sink, grabbing a glass from the cabinet and quietly filling it with tap water. I leaned against the sink and drank the water, relishing in its cool, soothing liquid going down my throat. That's when I overheard a voice outside. As I listened, I realised it was Janice. I strolled to the door and listened again until the words were almost clear. I opened the door and saw Janice outside talking to somebody on the phone. Her eyes darted at me. It startled her. She screamed as her phone dropped out of her hand and on to the ground. Almost immediately. She bent down, grabbed her phone and picked it up looking for the off button.

"Who are you talking to this late?" I asked.

Janice laughed nervously. "It's the others in the resistance. I was trying to find out what the next step was going to be."

I thought about it for a second, as her words made little sense. Why would they be up at three in the morning? "Why are you talking to them outside like this?" I asked.

"I didn't want to wake anybody up. Obviously you can see everybody's still asleep." Her defensive tone caught me off guard. She quickly passed by me and ran inside the house.

"Janice!" I yelled after her, trying to make it loud enough for her to hear me but quiet enough that the others wouldn't.

Janice ran up the stairs. I closed the door behind me and ran after her. "Janice!"

"Shut up!" One man shouted out from the couch. His voice was tired and rugged.

I wasn't looking to make a scene but; it was disturbing the way Janice was behaving. Some things weren't making sense, and I needed to know what they were. I decided that I would talk to Robert about what happened in the morning. But for now, I was going to go back down to the basement and try to get some sleep.

When I went into the basement, my mom was sleeping. She was snoring loudly, and it reminded me of being back at home. It's funny how some of the most annoying and frustrating traits about people are what you miss the most when they're gone. It reminded me of my dad. Tears threatened to pour all over again. I put him out of my mind as I knew that I had to focus on what was happening in front of us. My mind began racing. Could it be possible that Janice isn't being honest with us? What if she isn't who we thought she was? Why did she run away like that? What if she's working for the other side?

My mind was racing away from me, and I committed to getting a grip. After all, Janice was the one who saved me from being murdered by the FBI and drove me to safety. Maybe it's nothing, maybe it's part of the plan that I'm not meant to know. I gave her the benefit of the doubt and drifted slowly off to sleep. Sometime later, a knock at the door woke me up.

"Come upstairs. We're gonna talk about our plans for tomorrow." Robert called out through the door.

"The Raid is happening tomorrow?" I asked.

"Yes, he replied."

"Where's Janice?" I asked as I opened the door to face him.

"She's still in bed. Why do you ask?"

"I saw her last night whispering to someone on her phone and it was a little suspicious. When I confronted her, she ran upstairs." I explained.

What do you mean?" Robert stopped, turned around and looked at me before turning to run up the stairs. I followed quickly behind him, running to catch up. We walked down the hallway toward Janice's room. Robert turned the knob and opened the door to find that she wasn't in it. Her bed was undisturbed and hadn't been slept in. Janice was gone.

Robert's eyes widened in a slow realisation of what was going on.I felt a surge of panic as the pit of my stomach threatened to empty its contents. This was bad. This was terrible. I saw the window wide open and ran over to it to look outside. Janice's car was nowhere to be found. I looked again around the room, hoping I was wrong, hoping that she hadn't abandoned us, but I noticed that all of her clothes were gone. Everything she owned was gone. Robert looked out the window and then back at me. As our eyes met, we both realized this was as bad as it looked.

I noticed a red laser light was on his stomach. It didn't register to me at first what it was,but as it moved up to his head forehead I realized it was a laser used on a weapon to track a target. "Robert, look out!" I screamed.

It was too late. Blood splattered all over the room and all over my face. Robert's lifeless body dropped to the ground. I screamed repeatedly to the horror that was unfolding in front of me. More gunshots followed, this time shooting at the house. I heard the ping of the bullets as they hit the wall behind me. I ducked and fell to the floor. The bullets were coming much too fast to be a simple pistol. It must have been a higher powered semi-automatic weapon. I held my hands over my head, trying to protect myself. I heard the chorus of screams upstairs as the others realized what was happening. It felt like forever until the bullets stopped. I crawled out of the doorway and went upstairs. The people were scrambling around as they grabbed their guns.

"Stay here, Marlene." The woman with the hat said. They took off through the front door, cocking their guns, getting ready for retaliation.

CHAPTER 29

I kept my head down and peeked outside. What I saw amazed me. Fifteen of our people stood outside, guns locked and loaded at the ready. Observing and watching. They slowly surrounded the perimeter of the area to see where the gunshots were coming from. They ran out into the middle of the field, unafraid of what they might find. I stared outside, looking for the shooter. Was he up high somewhere or across the street? I wasn't sure. Just then the gunshots started again. I saw my new friends, the team of people in the revolution that was supposed to help us, get gunned down in the middle of the field in front of the house.

Terror swept over me. There was nobody left to help us. It was a surreal feeling. Like I was living in a nightmare that wouldn't end and I couldn't wake up no matter how hard I tried. Robert was dead and now all of these good kind-hearted people, too. I couldn't help but feel guilty. If it were not for me, maybe they would still be here. I screamed in horror and ran downstairs.

"Mom! Mom!" I shake her and screamed until she stirred out of her sleep. "Wake up, mom! We've got to go right now!"

"What's going on?" Her grogginess was fading.

I pulled her out of bed. "How could you not hear the shots?"

"I don't know. I feel so tired. What's going on?" My mother asked.

"They're all dead, mom. All of them. Robert and everyone else. They're gone!" I yelled trying not to get hysterical.

I pulled her to her feet and dragged her up the stairs to the first floor. I showed her "Look for yourself."

She looked outside and screamed.

"We don't have time for this. Put on your shoes. We've got to go right now." I yelled.

"Where's Robert?" My mom asked.

"I told you. He's dead. They're all dead. We are going to be next if we don't go."

Suddenly she understood the weight of the problem and quickly ran back to the basement, grabbed her shoes and her things. I followed her and collected my belongings and together we ran outside the back door and into the woods hoping that nobody saw us leave.

I could hear somebody coming through the bushes, rustling up the tall grass as they ran after us. "Keep running, mom!"

My mother is older, but she tried her best to keep up with

me. A bullet zoomed past my head and hit a tree. I remembered something I learned on the internet once that said if you're ever being fired at not to run in a straight line but in a zigzag pattern. I tried it and it was harder than I thought. When the bullet passed me, I ducked and screamed. My mom fell to the ground as she tripped on a tree root.

"Mom, let's go!" I turned around and helped her to her feet. We started running deep into the woods. The footsteps seemed to close in on us. I felt a pair of hands push me hard to the ground. A man in a suit with dark sunglasses wrestled with me as I fought and kicked him. He tried to get my hands pinned above my head but I turned and wriggled away.

"Get off my daughter!" My mom yelled as she hit the man on the head. She delivered blow after blow to the man.

Time slowed down as I watched her hit the man, impressed at my mother's agility to still fight off an attacker. I didn't know why that ran through my mind, but the surge of adrenaline put everything into slow motion. Another man ran up behind us and wrapped his arms around my mom, tackling her to the ground. She screamed and yelled before they threw her off her feet and stumbled backwards with the man on top of her. I got one good slap in on the man and then clawed his face, putting scratches over his forehead and nose. He yelped. I heard several other voices. There were men's voices, and they were running toward us.

"Hold her still." One man said.

"Hurry!" Another said.

I felt a sharp pain in my leg and realized that they injected me with something. My breathing was labored, and I was getting exhausted. My head grew foggy and my vision slowly faded to black.

CHAPTER 30

My head pounded against my skull as I slowly woke up and realized that I wasn't home. I wasn't in my bed. I wasn't in a safe spot. I was in what appeared to be a van. I tried moving my hand to bring it to my head, but I realized they tied me up. This looked familiar, and in fact, the van looked like the same van from last time. I tried to look around, but my vision was still a little blurry. As it cleared, I noticed that my mother was laying next to me asleep. They must have drugged us. The last thing I remembered was being in the woods with a team of men all around us.

A familiar voice toward the front passenger seat rang out. I turned, trying not to gain attention from anyone, but get a peek at who was sitting in the passenger seat. I confirmed my suspicions when I noticed Janice's brown hair.

My blood boiled seeing Janice. She had betrayed us all. And as a result, sixteen people were dead. I didn't want them to know that I had been awake, so I pretended to be asleep for the next several minutes. The van slowed down and then turned. I heard Janice and the driver talking. We were turning into a gas station. The driver put the van in park and turned off the ignition before leaving. I sat there looking at Janice. She was unaware that I was awake until she turned around and saw me looking at her.

"I'm so sorry, Marlene." Janice said.

"You betrayed us all. How can you live with yourself?" I asked.

"I had no choice." Janice's eyes started to tear up. "I'm so sorry."

"Where are we going?" I asked. "We're back in DC."

The door opened suddenly, as the driver got back in the van. I put my head down and pretended to be asleep so that he wouldn't notice. He turned the ignition on, put the van in reverse, pulled out of the parking lot and drove on. Janice turned around to take a quick look behind her and made eye contact with me. As I peeked to see what's going on, she had a guilty look in her eyes. She should have felt some remorse. She was responsible for making everything worse.

I wondered why we were in DC. I heard the familiar noise of traffic as we drove over the bridge. It was the Potomac. I put my head on the little window that separated me from the driver's seat and noticed that we were driving closer to the White House until I realized we were at the gate. The driver pulled up to the security guard and rolled down the window. "You got the girl?" He asked.

"Yeah, and her mom." The driver responded.

"Move on." The security guard waved him through. The van drove down the driveway.

"Why are we at the White House?" I asked.

"Shut up." The driver yelled back. He turned into a dark garage that seemed to go underground. He parked and after a minute opened the back of the van. There were several men in suits waiting. When the van doors opened, they grabbed me and my mom. One agent slung my mother over his shoulder. They made me walk with my hands tied behind my back. I saw Janice stay in the van as we were taken away. Where would they take us? And what would become of Janice?

I followed them, understanding that the only way to figure out how to get out of here was to comply for now. They led me to a door that had a lock on it. One agent typed a code on the door and put his fingerprint to be scanned on it. The door opened and inside was an elevator. I started shaking because I didn't know where we were going. I got nervous the deeper we went in that we would never come out.

We entered the elevator, and one agent pushed the button. It went down for what felt like ten minutes. We must have been going to the underground bunker that was created for the president in times of national security threats. The doors opened and I couldn't believe what I was witnessing. In a room were hundreds of girls on the ground chained up. The room extended like a long corridor. The girls watched me as they escorted me past them. It was strangely quiet. Tears fell from my eyes as I realized the horrifying truth. I was once again the victim of trafficking.

CHAPTER 31

They put my mother and I in a room separate from the rest of the girls. I didn't know why they made that decision, but I was grateful. I had already experienced that environment more than I ever wanted to in my life. While I was sorry and empathetic to those girls, I needed the time to think about how we were going to get out of here. The room was clean and white, and looked like they had used it for meetings.

It almost looked like it used to be an office, but the chairs and tables and everything that would adorn an office was taken out and the only thing that remained was carpet and walls.

Somehow my mom could sleep again. I didn't know if it was just because of all the trauma we had endured over the past few days. My father's death hit us both hard, but I knew that my mother depended on my dad for everything, especially emotional support. I wasn't sure what we would do from here on out without him. When she woke up, I told her everything about what had happened, how Janice had betrayed us and where we were.

"Mom, it's just so awful. This is exactly how it was when I was kidnapped before." My voice squeaked.

My mom reached out and pulled me to her. We embraced and held onto each other because that's all we had.

"This is a sick world we live in, Marlene. Whatever happens, just know that I love you." She squeezed me tight.

"I love you too, mom." We both cried as we held each other in the empty room.

The door opened suddenly and a man with a mask on walked in with a tray that contained a plate with two microwaved burritos. He sat it on the floor before backing out, shutting and locking the door behind him. There wasn't any time to react or overpower him.

My brain seemed to have been foggy and delayed from being able to make quick decisions. I looked at the food and then my mother. She picked it up and ate it. I took it away from her. "Don't eat this or anything that they bring you. How do you know they haven't drugged it?"

"But I'm hungry." She said.

"You'll be alright," I said. "Just don't eat or drink anything they have given you." I warned her.

"You know your father made me burritos all the time when we were first married and broke." My mother smiled at that memory.

"Oh really?" I offered.

"Yeah, he always made the times we struggled feel like an

exotic experiment." She laughed. "He'd tell me we were eating like the Aztecs ate long ago. I knew he was full of it, but I loved his imagination."

We spoke for a little while, comforting each other about the wonderful memories of my father. I fell asleep shortly after and awoke with a knock on the door that woke us out of our sleep. The door opened and a vast crowd of at least fifty women wearing blood red robes passed by the door. The man threw two red robes, matching the women walking by.

"Take your clothes off and put this on." He said.

"Where are we going? I demanded.

He ignored me and closed the door. My mom and I looked at each other, unsure what to do. We were supposed to take our clothes off, but that would not happen.

The same man opened the door again, only this time he had a gun pointed straight at us. Take your clothes off and put the robe on, " He demanded.

My mother nodded to me, showing that we should do what he said. We quickly took our clothes off except our underwear and put the robe on over it.

"No. Take all of your clothes off.

Again, my mom and I exchanged glances, embarrassed and humiliated at this already, but knew that he could kill us both if we didn't do as he demanded. We took off our underwear and threw them to the side. I fasten the red robe with the ties that were attached to it.

"Get out here," he demanded and waved the gun at us.

We both walked out the door into the crowd of women in robes. The man was careful to walk behind us.

"where are we going?" I asked again.

He didn't respond. He just looked straight ahead and urged us to move faster in front of him. If he would not answer me, then I would try to figure it out myself. Why did he want us to have red robes on? Why the color red? It dawned on me and my eyes widened as I remembered talking with Janice in the cabin in the woods. My breath caught in my throat as I realized this was a human sacrifice ritual ceremony under the White House.

He was leading us to our deaths. Quickly, I looked for any door that might be open or a way that we could escape. This long corridor didn't allow for any way but forward. There were so many women crowding the hallway that it was impossible to move. I started crying, feeling helpless and unsure of what to do. I just kept walking forward, knowing that my fate would be sealed if I continued to comply with these people. The women stopped at the end of the hallway in front of the large double door. The man pushed me through another door separating me from my mom.

"Mom!" I screamed.

My mom reached her hand out for me, but it was so fast that she couldn't grab me in time. The door closed behind me.

"Why did you separate us?" I screamed. "Let me see my mother!"

The man pushed me forward up a staircase. I hated I was crying, but my emotions were taking over and the fear was overwhelming me. It was a biological reaction. Inside, I was furious and hellbent on finding a way out of here. I climbed the stairs and reached the platform. There was a huge glass wall and on the other side of it a room full of people in black robes. I looked through the glass and saw a huge underground arena and a stage in the middle of it. There were hundreds of people in seats in the room, but I couldn't see their faces. It was extremely quiet. No one said a thing.

I looked behind me and realized I was the only one in this glass case room. I was the only one wearing red in a sea of black audience members. On the walls, I noticed there were pentagrams and other satanic symbols written in what looked to be blood. It carried over onto the ceiling. The audience members were sitting on couches facing each other. It was a gruesome sight. My knees shook from fear. It looked like I was the sacrificial lamb who was being led to the slaughter.

CHAPTER 32

The man who had guided me to the room at gunpoint left and shut the door, locking it behind him. Another man from across the room entered through the door and shut it behind him. "Nice to finally meet you, Marlene."

The voice behind the mask removed his hood and mask. His smile creeped me out. And then I recognized his face. It was Hullman. Terror swept through my body as adrenaline rushed through my veins. This was the man who tried to buy me in the beginning.

I said nothing, too terrified to move. My eyes darted

around the room, watching everybody stare at me through black hoods and masks. I heard a wave of laughter emanate over the room. Hulman took my arm as he guided me to the center of the room.

"Sit down." I did as he instructed and sat down on the ground in the center of the stage. They decorated it with a circle and a pentagram in the middle of it. The audience followed me with their eyes. "You have caused a lot of damage to your social media account. We are going to save you for last." Hullman laughed. "Ladies and gentlemen, reveal yourselves." Hullman instructed.

I watched the sea of people remove their masks. They took off their hoods and as they did; I realized that I knew a lot of them. Many of them were famous people I had seen several times on TV. There were politicians and a senator from Virginia. I saw the governor of California who waved at me with a sadistic mocking. I stood up, trying to see everybody's face. There were several news anchors who had called me a white supremacist on TV. When I looked

217

to the side of the audience, I saw my favorite singer who I had just been singing her song the other day. There was a talk show host who was the most popular celebrity in the world smiling at me. A famous rapper was standing next to her.

I could not believe these famous, well-known people were part of this sadistic cult. I felt defeated. If these people who we thought were the best of society were actually the worst, then what hope did we have of stopping this? Fear and panic gripped me. I lost control.

"Where am I?" I screamed?

The entire crowd laughed at me, unsympathetic to my situation. "Where's my mother?" I screamed.

The crowd continued laughing. Hullman spoke up. "Ladies and gentlemen, give us a round of applause for this year's sacrifice." The entire crowd burst into applause, cheering as if they were at a sporting event. It was as if their favorite player was about to conquer the winning shot.

Hullman began chanting in Latin as the crowd burst out in whispers. It was eerie and evil, and I did not know how to escape it or if I could.

I jerked as an enormous ball of fire lit up on stage behind me with a satanic symbol of a goat's head which caught on fire. The audience began chanting with Hullman. Their voices grew louder. Hullman let out a tremendous scream and the entire room followed him screaming from the top of their lungs. And almost as quickly, the room went silent again.

I clasped my hands to my chest, not understanding what was happening. I looked around the room as the people in the audience were on their knees. I turned around and in the corner of the room, I saw Janice standing there. She looked back at me and my eyes widened as she looked exactly like one of the audience members dressed in a black robe. Janice nodded and pointed her eyes toward the closet door. Then locked eyes with me again. I didn't understand what she was doing, but it seemed as if she was signalling me somehow.

The audience rose to their feet. "Please be seated, ladies and gentlemen." Hullman said. He sauntered to the back of the stage in the shadows and brought out a girl in a red robe that was dressed like me. I was confused, but the girl's face looked even more confused. I watched her Hullman brought her to the center of the stage next to me. There was a moment of pause. I wasn't sure what was happening.

Hullman reached from inside of his robe, pulled out a sharp, long dagger that gleamed in the stage lights and without warning, stabbed the girl in her throat. Blood muddled her screams that squirted from her neck. He let her go, and she stumbled and fell to the ground, blood pouring out involuntarily from her throat. Another figure walked up to Hullman with a wineglass in his hand.

Hullman took it from the man and bent down next to the girl. He dug the knife deeper in her neck and then placed the wineglass under her neck and collected the pouring blood. As the girl slowly drifted into unconsciousness, the thick, red substance filled the cup. When the wine glass was full, he held it in the air. The crowd cheered as the girl laid there lifeless. I saw her vacant eyes. There was no spirit left in it. I scooted back, crawling away from this atrocity. Hullman drank the blood from the glass. Part of the stage opened up to reveal a fire pit below. Hullman grabbed the girl's lifeless body and threw it into the fire pit.

CHAPTER 33

Blood thickly coated the stage floor. The more I scrambled to get away from the violent scene, the more I slipped. The vile rose in my throat and I wanted to vomit all over the stage. I was still trying to process what had just happened. How did all of this happen? And how could somebody as prominent as Hullman be allowed to do this in front of hundreds of people without consequence? I couldn't believe what I had just witnessed. I couldn't believe how big this underground operation actually was.

"Bring out the others." Hullman commanded. This time

the girls were all naked with chains on their hands and linked to each other. They stood in the middle of the stage, trembling. I had crawled to the edge of the glass wall and could do nothing but shake, knowing what was about to happen and not being able to stop it. Hullman used the same knife to cut a second girl's throat. The other girls screamed as it forced them to look on, unable to do anything. Blood squirted everywhere. I looked at the audience and realized that a line had formed. Each audience member held a wine glass, taking turns trying to catch the blood with their glass. The other girls who were chained to the girl who had been cut, were screaming but were held down by additional people in the audience who had come up into the stage.

Some of the audience members brought their own sacrificial knives. Hullman recited a chant in Latin. when he was finished. The same six people stabbed the remaining six girls in the neck. Their screams were horrifying. I couldn't get them out of my head. All the girls collapsed to the ground. Like vampires, the audience members collected the blood of these girls in their wine glasses. When they had gotten their fill, they raised their glasses to the audience and drank it. The audience cheered in reaction.

I collapsed to the ground, crying at the realization of knowing that I was next. Nobody had any compassion for these women or myself. I knew I would suffer the same fate as these girls.

"Burn them my good patrons." Hullman gave the command and the same audience members who had cut their throats, threw them into the fire pit. They all chanted as they watched the girls burn. I broke out into a hysterical crying jag, unable to stop. The people in the room formed a line to leave. The room emptied. I looked back up and I was alone. I got up and more ran toward where I saw the others leave, but there was a man with a gun in front of the door. I could see him through the glass.

The closet door opened, and Janice came out. "Marlene, help me get this out." Janice said as she grunted.

I walked toward her. "What is it?"

"It's a portable news camera." She said.

"How'd you get that in here?" I asked.

"My uncle runs Channel Seven news. I stole the camera this morning." She pulled the camera out of the closet as I helped her.

"I used my parents' White House pass to get down here." Janice flipped on the camera.

"You betrayed me!" I yelled.

"I'm on your side, Marlene. They followed us to the house, and I didn't have a choice. They were going to find out that I was part of the resistance if I hadn't turned you in." She explained. "They would have shot into the house regardless, Marlene. You have to believe me."

I didn't believe her. I didn't know what to believe anymore.

Another scream came from the stage as another group of girls were murdered. I didn't have a choice. I had to trust her for now. I helped Janice take the camera and tripod out and place it in front of the window, aiming it toward the stage. They seemed to have forgotten about me amid their blood hungry thirst for sacrificial victims. They didn't see me helping Janice.

Janice ran to the door entrance to barricade it. I helped her by putting a sofa on the front door. The gunman heard everything happening inside the room, but did nothing.

"Don't worry, Marlene. He's on our side." Janice said, panting hard.

We continued to barricade the door with furniture. I heard another scream from the stage as a third set of girls were being murdered. I didn't think I would ever get the sound of these terrified, screaming girls out of my head. I was horrified that my mother and I would be next.

CHAPTER 34

Janice's watch started beeping. "C'mon Marlene!"

"I'm coming," I replied.

Janice stood by the news camera and clicked the record button. The camera's red light lit up. Janice's phone rang, and she picked it up.

"We're Live!" I heard a girl yell from the other end of Janice's phone. Janice zoomed the camera in as the fourth set of nude girls entered the stage. The next six people in black robes who were waiting in line took off their hoods. Janice scanned over to Hullman's face. He grabbed the same blood-soaked knife he'd used to kill the first girl and stabbed another the girl, this time on her breast. She let out a scream of pain as Hullman continued to plunge the knife into her repeatedly. Once the girl stopped squirming and fell to the floor, he bent over her and drank from the hole he created in the top of her breast. The crowd chanted in Latin.

"We have two million viewers from home, Janice!" The girl on the phone yelled.

"Good." Janice replied.

My eyes widened as hope filled my spirits again. Maybe revealing all of this to the world would save us. Maybe this was what it would take to take this whole cult down. A huge boom sound shook the ground from above. The audience stopped the killings and looked up.

"It's them," Janice whispered with a grin on her face and turned the camera on herself. "Good evening, America and the rest of the world. What you are seeing is Satanic Worship of the global elite coming to you live under the

White House!" Janice said, looking at the camera.

I felt so much relief that the truth was finally being revealed. No more would anyone doubt that what I had been through was true. No more would anyone give me strange looks or call me weird. They validated me beyond all questioning, and Janice made all of this happen.

Suddenly, shots rang out in the room. Panic set in and the audience members screamed and tried running from the room. The people of the revolution charged in, shooting the black-robed audience members. Others with Q Anon, confederate flags, along with other far right flags. The security surrounding Hullman pulled out their guns and shot back, but were gunned down. They filled the air with the smell of blood and gunpowder. I kept my head down until the shooting stopped. When I finally looked up, I saw Janice laying next to me smiling.

"We're safe here, Marlene," said Janice.

"What about my mom?" I asked.

"We will find her." Janice helped me up to my feet and then grabbed her camera. It was still recording a live stream. She panned around the room watching the rebels handcuffing surviving members of the audience. They tried to get them out of the room but had trouble navigating around the dead bodies that covered the floor.

CHAPTER 35

The twenty girls who were sacrificed laid burning in the pit in front of the stage. The flames rising. The stench was unbearable, and I tried my best not to vomit. I covered my mouth with my hand, trying not to breathe as much as possible. A giant sigh of relief overcame me and I took a second to give a silent prayer of thanks that I survived. What was going to happen to us now? Where would we go from here?

"Marlene! Marlene! Help!" I heard my mother screaming my name as I heard someone coming down the stairs. My stomach dropped. I ran toward the stairs and the sound of my mother's voice, removing the furniture Janice and I had used to barricade the door.

"Wait! Let me help you." Janice ran up beside me and helped me move the furniture.

Once the furniture was moved, I opened the door to see that the gunman who was guarding the door was shot dead. Hullman stood there with his arm around my mother's neck and a knife to her throat. "You! You did this!" Hullman yelled between his teeth, enraged. He stayed at the doorframe of the room and began chanting in Latin.

"Mom noo!" I ran toward them as fast as I could.

Hullman grabbed the knife and stabbed my mom in the thigh. My mother screamed in pain as the blood dripped down her leg. She wriggled around as Hullman returned the sharp blade to her neck. I stood there in horror, unable to move any closer for fear that he would kill her. And that's when it happened. A gunshot rang out from behind me as a single bullet entered Hullman's forehead. He fell to the ground as my mother fell, clutching her wound. I ran over to her and pressed my hand on it to stop the bleeding.

I looked over and saw Janice standing on the stairs, her arms outstretched with a gun in her hand. "Are you both okay?"

I looked up at her in awe and with a newfound respect. "Yes, I think my mother will be fine. Thank you, Janice."

I heard more rebels run up the stairs with Q Anon shirts and Trump attire to help my mother. "We will take care of your mother, don't worry." The man named Mike took off his Q Anon shirt and tied it around my mom's leg to stop the bleeding.

Mike picked up my mother, stepped over Hullman's dead body, and ran down the stairs as I followed close behind. "I'm here, mom. I'm right behind you." I turned around and stared back at Janice. "Thank you, Janice."

Janice nodded as she picked up the news camera. "Go be

with your mom. I got it from here."

I smiled and ran down the stairs after Mike and my mom. There was huge infighting and chaos in the audience below. Hundreds of men with guns wearing Trump and Q Anon shirts were still fighting those who were still in their black robes.

I followed Mike, who ran across the room and into the entrance tunnel past the enormous crowd of people surging into the stage. We struggled on the side of the tunnel, trying to go the opposite way. After six minutes of struggling, we made it to the end of the tunnel and pressed the up key on the elevator. We waited as hundreds of rebel men and a few women poured down the staircase beside the elevator. The elevator opened and about fifty men squeezed in the elevator poured out into the tunnel to the arena. It was empty as nobody was going up.

We got in and pressed the button to go up. The doors closed. "Marlene, I feel tired." My mom's eyes grew heavy.

I could hear my mom panting from the deep cuts in her thigh. I tried not to lose my focus. I wanted to get hysterical about my mother's injury, or the horrific scenes I had witnessed tonight. I wanted to curl up in a ball and cry for a month. But I was just so grateful it was over. It was finally all over.

"It's alright, mom. We're going to get you to a hospital." I assured her.

"We did it," Marlene's mother smiled.

"Yes, we did." Marlene smiled back.

CHAPTER 36

The elevator reached the top, and the doors opened. Fifty more men were ready to enter as we were trying to get out. Mike held onto my mom and motioned for me to follow him out of the elevator and into the basement of the White House. I could hear screams and shots echoing through the basement. It was complete chaos. We ran out of the basement into the streets of DC. There were what appeared to be miles of Q Anon flags, confederate flags, and people screaming. News helicopters were flying overhead everywhere. Fire, smoke, and rioting spread all over the streets of DC..

I rushed to Mike's side. "What is all of this?"

"We stormed the white house after it went live on the news." Mike said.

I looked into a bar and saw there were twenty people huddled in front of the screen. The television showed Janice's face and then the satanic ritual of girls being killed and thrown into the pit. The camera turned and showed my face. My eyes widened as I realized I was once again the center of national news.

I noticed several people stopping what they were doing to stare at me. I still wore the red robe I was given. I tried to look down so that nobody noticed me and put my hood on my head. We walked for six blocks with my mother being carried by Mike. I noticed people had their phones out, taking pictures of me. I wasn't sure why there was so much interest, but I continued on trying to ignore them. We walked past looters and people screaming about pedophiles and Q Anon. I saw another television that was on in a small store. It showed the president of the United States in handcuffs wearing a black robe. It shocked me to see the president in handcuffs being walked out of the elevator I just went up.

The three of us walked into a downstairs parking garage and got into Mike's pickup truck. As we drove out, I saw small stores were being looted as we drove by. Part of me felt sorry for the small business owners. They did nothing wrong, and now their livelihoods were being destroyed. I tried not to think about it and focus on our escape. Washington, DC, was in total chaos and anarchy. There were no police in sight. It looked like the people had overpowered them. As we drove away from the White House, I saw a fiery blaze in the rearview mirror and realized it had been set ablaze. Despite that, there were people running inside and looting it.

"Mom, are you alright?" I asked, noticing that she was smiling.

"I'm okay. I think the bleeding is under control." She said.

The bloody Q Anon shirt was wrapped around her thigh.

CHAPTER 37

We drove over the Potomac River and out into the DC suburbs. Mike drove for a while until he saw a hospital. He followed the signs for the emergency entrance and pulled up to it. He turned off the truck, got out and walked around to the other side where my mom was. He grabbed my mother and carried her inside. The entire hospital staff looked at me and then back to the television, noticing that my face kept showing up on their screen. I worried what people would do once they knew it was me on the screen. I brushed that thought from my mind for now. The only focus that concerned me should be on my mother and her recovery. I watched as the hospital staff put my mother into a bed and rolled her into a room. I sat in the emergency room waiting for an update.

"Hey, I gotta go back to DC. Need anything?" Mike asked.

I shook my head. "You have done more than enough for my mother and myself. There is no way I can repay you for your help and kindness."

"Are you kidding? After everything you've done for the cause, it was the least I could do." He smiled, and I noticed for the first time the dimples in his cheeks.

"Please be safe on your travels." I said.

Mike left and as I sat in the emergency room, I thought about all that had happened and how we all ended up here. There was so much loss that we'd all experienced and not much time to process it. I knew there would come a time when I would need to grieve the loss of my father and the friends I'd lost. So far, I'd had to stay in survival mode. That was the safest place for me to be right now. Constantly watching and waiting for the end of this nightmare.

I sat in the emergency room, still with my red robe on. Hospital staff crowded around me. At first, I wasn't sure if I was noticing it, but when people started coming up to me and asking questions, I knew they were interested in what I had to say. Questions turned into taking pictures of me and with me. It felt strange. I got up and tried to walk away, but the staff followed me. It began to get uncomfortable. I was worried about my mother and wanted to focus on her. One of the staff saw how uncomfortable I was and let me into an empty room. "Can you let me see my mother?"

"Sure, follow me." They guided me into a room where my mother was resting peacefully, her leg bandaged up.

"Thank you so much." I said to the nurse.

She smiled and nodded before closing the door behind her. I walked over to my mom's bed and sat down on the chair next to her. "Mama, how are you doing?"

She opened her eyes and smiled at me. "You're a hero," she

said.

"Not hardly." I protested. "It was Mike who got us here."

"I would like to thank him. Where is he?" She asked.

"He went back to carry on the fight."

The door opened and the same nurse who had just helped me returned. "I brought you some clothes. I thought you'd like to change."

"Thank you so much." I said.

"Come up here." My mom patted the empty half of the mattress beside her. "Come get in bed like you used to when you were a little girl."

I smiled and climbed in next to her. We spoke about better times. Mornings sitting around the breakfast table eating with dad. Tears streamed down my face as I held my mother and said a silent prayer of gratitude for all that we still had. I fell asleep for the first time in months feeling safe.

CHAPTER 38

3 weeks later.

The house felt so cold and empty since he's been gone. It used to have a lovely colorful joy about it. The kind of a rainbow explosion that would hit you as soon as you opened the front door. All those days I came home from school and took the beauty and splendor of it for granted, tugged at my aching heart. I would never get that time back. I would never get another day to tell my father how much I loved him. How much of a hero he was to me. I would never get another chance to hold his hand, or to have him walk me down the aisle on my wedding day. My daddy was gone forever.

I brushed a falling tear away from my face and lifted my eyes upward so that more wouldn't follow. I didn't want to feel this pain. I didn't want my mother, who had spent the past three weeks pretending her heart wasn't broken, to have to endure it any longer either. I wished and prayed above anything else that we could go back to a time before my father's murder. But I would not waste another day on foolish fantasies. I had my mother to take care of and a new life to build for us both.

I stood in front of my silver-framed full-length mirror and gazed at my dress. It was black with lace around the collar and sleeves. I brushed my hair back with a headband that kept my hair out of my face. If I could get through this day without breaking down in front of God and everybody, I would consider it a small miracle.

"Oh sweetheart. You look beautiful. Your father would be so proud of you." My mother startled me. She stood in the doorway.

"Thank you, mom. I'm so sorry that we are here." I apologized. I knew it was my fault my father was dead. Just like I knew it was my fault that so many others had died. I didn't know how I would forgive myself or if I even deserve forgiveness.

"Oh sweetheart. You're not responsible for what happened to your father. There's nothing you could have done to stop any of it. Please don't spend your life blaming yourself." My mother's eyes watered as she took a tissue from her pocket and dabbed at the corners.

"I guess we should go." I said.

We walked into the hallway, grabbed the keys to the car and locked the house. My brother Mark had returned from college for the funeral. He was suffering a lot and was still mad at my father's death. I wasn't sure how to talk with him about it. I didn't know if he blamed me. Lord knows, I blame myself.

"I missed you, Mark." I offered. My brother was several years older than me, so we really never had much to say. He lived an entirely different life away at college, and we didn't get to spend much time together. Still, it was comforting to have him here.

"I missed you too, Marlene. How are you holding up?" He asked.

"As well as expected, I suppose." I tried to smile, but my mouth could only produce a straight line.

"It's okay, sis. You don't have to pretend with me." He wrapped his arms around me and I held onto him for at least a full minute. It was the closest my brother, and I had been in years. I sniffled into his chest. "I think it's time to go."

I pulled away from him, grabbed my purse and headed out the door. The whole way to the funeral home we didn't speak. The air was so thick that it felt hard to breathe. Just the thought of making polite conversation was exhausting.

I dreaded having to have this service. I would have been happier to pay my respects to my dad in private. But this was what you did when someone you loved died. You gave everyone who knew him an opportunity to speak about how they felt about him. That part might be nice to sit through and listen. I was interested to know how many people's lives my dad touched.

We pulled up to the funeral home. I saw several news vans and television cameras parked out front and on the lawn. I knew this would be difficult. I didn't want to answer the reporters' questions; not today.

"Follow me and stay close," Mark took off his blazer and put it around my head. He helped me out of the car and then helped my mom.

As we walked through the sea of news people, I saw Janice and Mike out of the corner of my eye. The followed us into the funeral home. I was glad to have them there with me. We'd all been through so much. It was important that we all got closure.

The funeral service was touching. I was glad despite my earlier reservations about it, I went. There were so many more people who showed up than I had anticipated, and it felt good knowing that my father was so well loved. We went home to prepare for the reception, where only family and close friends were invited. I trudged around the house listlessly, not really paying attention to the conversations going on around me. My thoughts were on my father and how much I missed him, and how life would now never be the same again.

"Hi Marlene." A voice behind me broke the silence of my own thoughts.

I turned around to see who was speaking, and it was a man in an expensive suit. He wasn't immediately recognizable to me, but he looked like an important official of some sort.

"Please allow me to extend my condolences to you and your family. I'm so sorry for losing your father." He extended his hand to shake mine. "We haven't met. I'm Deputy Director of the CIA, Charles Wagner." I extended my hand to shake with his. "Do you have a minute to talk?"

I nodded my head, too emotionally exhausted to care too much.

"First, let me say that you are a hero. On behalf of my organization and many others, we want to thank you for your bravery. You managed to bust up an extensive trafficking ring among other major organized crime networks that we have been trying to take down for over a decade." He released my hand and motioned for us to move into the next room and sit down. "You are a hero."

"I don't feel like one." I objected.

"Because of you, many people are in jail tonight. You should be proud of yourself." He said.

"I don't feel much like celebrating." I said.

"The president was impeached within three hours and many congress persons were jailed, too."

"What about Janice's parents?" I asked.

"They were arrested as well. Janice helped us by explaining what had been happening in her home for some time. As a result, we were able to expose the large scale sex trafficking ring across the world. Marlene, you need to understand — this is huge."

"What about Dmitri?" I asked. I especially wanted to know what happened to him and his parents since they started me on all this.

"He and his parents were taken into custody trying to get into Russia. They have plastered their faces all over the news for the last forty-eight hours. They will be extradited to the US to face charges. Would you be willing to testify in court?" He asked.

"Yes. I will do whatever I can to ensure they never do this to anyone else." I said.

"Many world leaders were jailed. Very famous and influential people were put into handcuffs. It was a crazy witch hunt on TV and social media." Things will be hot for a while, but we've finally got enough evidence to put them all away for a very long time. Thanks to you." Wagner stood up and shook her hand again. "We'll be in touch."

I grabbed my phone and logged into my social media. I found that I had gained over one million followers. The live video feed had spread everywhere, including mainstream news. Everyone was talking about it, but all I wanted was to forget about it all. I scrolled through the top news stories and saw that S.W.A.T. teams all across the country had stormed hundreds of homes freeing kidnapped women and girls who had been kept in chains and sometimes much worse. It was like a domino effect and it was in full motion. I couldn't believe so many kids in my school were aware that this was happening, but did nothing about it. I was sure it terrified them, but now their families were being arrested.

Over the next several days, I had countless requests to speak to the news media, but I didn't want any of it. I was tired of being the poster girl for trafficked girls. I wanted to focus on learning how to rebuild my life. My mom, brother, and I attended family counseling, and I also attended individual counseling. I didn't want this experience to shape the rest of my life, or have a hold on me. I needed to learn how to manage my fear and move forward.

CHAPTER 39

"The nation owes you a debt of gratitude," the President of the United States told me over the phone. He had just been sworn in as president after his predecessor was arrested with the conspiracy to run an international trafficking ring. "We thank you from a grateful nation for your sacrifice to save so many."

"Thank you, Mr. President." I said.

"Would you and your family please join me at the White House next week? We would like to present you with the Presidential Medal of Freedom." The president asked.

I was hesitant. This was too much. I didn't feel like a hero, or like anyone who deserved a medal. All I did was survive my horrible captivity. I looked over at my mom, who was listening in. She shook her head profusely to show that I should accept the president's offer. I looked over at Janice, who gave me a thumbs up. "It would be an honor, Mr. President."

"Great! My social secretary will contact you to set it all up. Thank you again, Marlene, for your sacrifice and courage." The phone clicked, and I heard a dial tone.

The honor was great, but I would be happy when the world moved on to other things. When the time came to accept the medal, they were still cleaning up the city after the rioting. There had been so much damage to the city that the president had to declare an emergency just to help rebuild it.

After the ceremony, I posted on my social media again. It had been the first time in months and my following had increased to ten million subscribers. Something was born in me after all of this happened. I newfound courage I never had before. I had the courage to speak out on social media and started telling my followers that I was okay and talking to them about what I was learning in therapy.

My mom decided this story needed to be told, so she hired a ghostwriter to come and visit with me twice a week. She would listen to my story and take notes. I found it very helpful coming to terms with my trauma. We became pretty good friends over the time we spent together.

A few months later, I graduated high school and was accepted into college with a full ride scholarship. Life was slowing down gradually. Not as many reporters at my front door anymore. I was glad for that. Glad for the quiet and the time to hear myself think. What would I tell my children about my dad? How would I be able to convey how much he loved me and how much he would have loved them? A streak of sorrow overcame me for an instant at the thought. I missed him every day, but I knew he was in a better place. I knew I would one day see him again.

I released my book about the whole incident and could sell one million copies in two days through pre-order sales. It was unbelievable. Everyone wanted to know what happened and if they might know of someone who was involved. It was such a massive operation that it was likely almost everyone in the country knew someone who knew someone who was involved.

I'm just an ordinary girl who had something unusual and extraordinary happen to her. I'm nothing special. It could have happened to anyone.

But it didn't. It happened to me.

Made in United States
North Haven, CT
26 February 2024

49217151R10143